THE CENTURION
She-Wolf – Book 2

Diana Philbrick

THE CENTURION
She-Wolf – Book 2

FETISH WORLD BOOKS

A FETISH WORLD BOOKS PAPERBACK

ISBN: 978 1 78695 707 8

FETISH WORLD BOOKS
is an imprint of
Fiction4All
This Edition Published 2021

Introduction

She knew what to expect, they had whipped her before.

Although experience didn't make it any easier. If anything, knowing what to expect increased her tension. She shook off the tremors that were shaking her body…she had no intention of letting the Romans see her fear.

Her fear…

It's okay, she told herself. Any sane person would fear the *ferula* especially when a strong man wielded it. She could not remember the pain the last time the centurion had whipped her, only the writhing, the loss of control, the shame at showing weakness, but there was nothing she could do to prevent it—when Metella ordered it, she suffered.

The worst part of a whipping was Viper touching her. The despicable Sergeant Vipsanius enjoyed her agony, her shame, her body. He had stripped her and tied her naked between two tall wooden posts…spayed open like a farm animal ready for slaughter. She could see the lust in his eyes as his men tied the ropes on her wrists, as they lifted her feet off the ground and spread her legs, tying her ankles to the uprights.

He was the worst, but this kind of punishment was not unusual. The Romans were all cruel; eschewing reason when it came to captives and relying almost exclusively on the threat of corporal punishment to control those they had subjugated…and it worked. Many of the Briton slaves they had taken, some fierce warriors before their capture, would tremble and piss themselves if they somehow displeased their masters. They were truly defeated, she thought, beaten into submission; now, they were no more than Roman pets and beasts for the romans to work to death. Slavery was at the heart of their "enlightened" civilization.

She would never become the Roman centurion's pet. She had agreed to translate for him, but she had not surrendered…she had never surrendered, and she never would. She hated Rome and all Romans were her enemy; killing them was her *raison d'etre*, her purpose in life. It was the reason she continued to resist their dominance.

Which was why she was here. Despite their agreement regarding translation, the centurion continued to act as her master, and she continued to resist his domination. The result was frustration for him and the pain of frequent punishment for her like today. She hated the pain and despised him for subjecting her to such suffering, but she also understood the need to maintain the roles their fragile relationship demanded—she could not submit, and he could not allow her opposition to go unpunished.

It didn't matter, she thought, shaking her head. To her, the more punishment he decreed, the more he was admitting his inability to tame her. She was still fighting, still battling the hated invaders who had attacked her village, butchered her father, and crucified her mother in retaliation. She had died slowly, looking at Xara the entire time with a stare that said only one thing—avenge us! What were a few lash strokes compared to that sacred mission…?

A few lash strokes...

Even though he assigned her bondage to Viper, Metella always punished her himself and used his considerable strength to ensure that the whip struck her body with full force and effect. She knew he would not whip her to death as the Romans liked to do with others. He needed her to translate the Briton tongues into Latin and vice versa so that he could win cheap victories for Rome through negotiation. He would not jeopardize that goal. Nor would he scar her with his whip. He enjoyed her long lean body, her high tits and ass, her face too much.

No, she was not concerned for her life or her appearance. Even the pain, the excruciating agony of the leather slapping her raw skin was something she tolerated without complaint. What did bother her was looking weak in front of her enemies. Weakness would bring dishonor to her parents and her tribe. She would rather he slit her throat than shame them.

Then there was the other matter. When he fucked her, the centurion made her come like no one ever had done before. Even Caratacus, the chief of the Catuvellauni and her erstwhile lover, had not made her scream with the pain and pleasure of sexual climax the way the Roman did. Of course, Caratacus had never wanted her to use her mouth fearing the same fate as the Lucius Flaccus, the legate who had tried to rape her in Rumabo.

The centurion, Metella, did not have the same concern of course since he did not know about her private battle with Flaccus. He had only the natural caution of a master to an untamed slave; when he wanted to fuck her in the mouth, he used a slave's ring gag. The ring gag did not lessen the frequency or volume of his ejaculations—he apparently enjoyed the autonomic efforts of her lips and tongue, the soft feel of her throat, the warmth of…

The sound of Roman sandals on stone ended her erotic daydream. She would need to steel herself now, marshal all her Taexali strength, focus all her hatred on her Roman nemesis to cope with the suffering she was about to endure.

This whipping will be good for me, she told herself. It is exactly what I need to burn away any affection she might have for this Roman. She was only allying herself with him to save others from his cruelty; she enjoyed his cock and felt ecstasy climaxing with him because she was a woman, and he was a man. She would feel the same with any man. There was nothing personal in it, and one day, she would take her revenge on him.

"LEAVE US…!" Metella screamed at the leering Viper.

He waited until the sergeant was gone then put his hand on her cunt and put his mouth close to her ear.

"You have brought this on yourself, Xara. I cannot have a slave ignore my orders. It undermines my authority with my men. You must obey and respect me! If not, I have no choice but to…to hurt you."

"I will do as I have promised, *Ignavus*," she hissed, her labia throbbing in his hand, "but as long as you wear that uniform, I cannot obey or respect you."

"This is not a uniform, Xara. This is who I am."

He stepped back and laid a vicious stroke on her back then continued the merciless attack until she groaned. But it was not from the pain, it was from the dilemma of simultaneously despising and admiring someone with such intensity.

Chapter One - Negotiari

The centurion sat tall on his horse. Xara ran behind tethered to his saddle's pommel. Behind them, a mounted adjutant pulled a naked gift-slave named Yoanie, whom he had also tethered to his saddle. From a distance, the slaves looked like sleek greyhounds running alongside the imposing backdrop of huge Roman war horses. Marcus hoped that the Atrebates would view two riders leading two beautiful slaves as peaceful.

Metella's eyes were locked on the trail ahead, drilling into the darkness as if he could see what lay beyond. From overheard camp gossip, she had learned that this was the farthest north that any Roman soldier had ever ventured in Briton. She believed it; the Roman's had focused their conquests on the south, but with the demand for slaves rising throughout the empire, they had to expand. She kept glancing at Metella, wondering if he saw what she saw in the trees.

Her father had told her about the Great Northern Forest, about the fierce Atrebates Tribe that claimed exclusive ownership of the forest and everything it contained, about how the Atrebates enforced this claim by murdering anyone who ventured into their domain and by hanging their dissected body parts from tree limbs. This gruesome warning had become their signature.

He also spoke about other tribes that lived beyond the forest—the Carvetii, the Selgovae, the

Votadini, and the Picts—but he never lingered long on the Picts. She had always had the feeling that talking about them made him uncomfortable…even afraid…which was astonishing to her. This man had faced wolves with only a knife, he had killed eleven of the Romans who attacked their village, he had even managed to kill the spearman who had run him through. Her irrational, inherited fear of the Picts stemmed from his.

There were no Picts in the forest though, only Atrebates, who were nearly as terrifying.

The forest itself was intimidating—dark, full of tall and dense pine trees that hid the sky and the trail. It was as if they were traveling inside a small bubble of light. She found her inability to see the sky or the horizon especially disorienting—there was no way to navigate, no reference points to latch onto, no shadows, only the black tunnel-like hole that distinguished the forest trail from the trees. Xara remembered that she had been trying to reach this labyrinth after escaping from the Romans at Rumabo Imperium. She was fortunate that Caratacus had rescued her before she got to the forest; she would have been helpless in here. The Atrebates would have killed her.

She looked up at Metella again trying to shake off the dread she felt. The forest was like a great bear swallowing them alive. The thought made her stand still for a moment until the tether around her wrists jerked her forward. She ran forward until the rope was slack, and the centurion's horse swung his tail into her face as if annoyed with her.

Xara quickly advanced another two paces until she was beside Metella's stirrup, out of range of the animal's tail. She was sweating from the day's run, and the errant streaks of light that made it through the trees were glistening off her nearly naked body. The Romans had replaced her loin cloth with three leather belts—one around her neck, a collar, one around her breasts, and a third around her waist. A long and thin strip of leather extended from the front of her collar, between her legs, and up to the back of her collar in the nape of her neck. It rubbed against her clit as she ran and occasionally precipitated a minor orgasmic shudder. It wasn't an orgasm, more like a release of pent-up arousal, but it amused the mastiff running free at her side. On Metella's orders, the Romans had left the gift-slave Yoanie naked except for her wrist binding. Romans didn't waste cloth on their dogs or horses, why would they waste it on their slaves?

Xara's theory about the belts she wore was that the centurion wanted to expose her body, thereby marking her as a slave, but he also wanted to give her some stature over Yoanie, the gift slave. In his mind, Xara would be able to function with more credibility as his official translator if he elevated her some.

It was clever, she thought, another indication that he was a more sophisticated thinker than his rank implied. The Atrebates chief would probably feel insulted if the Roman used a common sex slave to translate. According to the gossip she had overheard, Metella was now officially the legion's chief negotiator. A soldier as chief negotiator…, she thought? Somehow the idea of it didn't sit right with her. Still, he was an imposing figure on his high horse with her tethered behind and his dogs at this side.

Their dogs…

Metella owned a pair of magnificent mastiffs that ran untethered behind and alongside his horse. Xara had already formed a bond with them; they reminded her of the fierce dogs she lived with under Sextus the torturer at Rumabo. They could rip out an enemy's throat or snap his neck with a ferocity that struck fear into the hearts of all who faced them. For her though, they were in a way her people; now that the Taexali were gone, and even the Catuvellauni, whom did she have left to call family? The other slaves, the Romans…? She would never be one of them, never!

One of the dogs running at her side bumped his large skull into her bare thigh and she pushed him away with her hip. He was an ugly beast for sure, with a short coat, a long low-set tail, and drooping pendant-shaped ears. Even if he and his brother were not family, they were the closest she had to friends. Metella turned his head quickly to the side and looked down to watch them running together. His stern expression didn't change.

Metella...

Ever since the incident in the horse pen when Metella had coerced her into agreeing to translate, she had been wary of him. He was not just strong, skilled, and ruthless, he was clever. He had made her a coconspirator in his battle against Princess Ailios, Caratacus's daughter. That had been his goal all along; he didn't care about Ailios or the seven other slaves he crucified. It was all about aligning her with him.

Her anger over his manipulation boiled up suddenly and she pulled on the rope holding her wrists to the saddle. Metella glanced down again then turned back to the front unbothered by her sudden unexplained pique. Roman masters didn't concern themselves with the feelings of their slaves unless those feelings affected them in some way.

Xara fumed at the memory of the horse pen for another minute then glanced back at Yoanie. The girl was pretty—soft, short, and well-built, with exaggerated tits and a jutting ass—just the kind of woman the Romans would assume a savage like Verica, the chief of the Atrebates, would enjoy owning…and fucking. Metella had not shared any of the details of their mission with her, but she had filled in the details from the bits and pieces she overheard.

The Romans typically spoke freely around Briton slaves whom the assumed did not understand Latin. It was something they did around her as well out of habit even though most now knew she spoke their language

She glanced at the centurion again, wondering if he knew the Atrebates were watching, following them invisibly from the depths of the forest. Xara could smell them; she hoped after years of fighting that his sixth sense for danger was equally sharp. In a bow to Roman tradition rather than any conviction that it would protect them, he held a *tregua vexillum* (flag of truce) in his stirrup. She was not sure that the Atrebates even knew what the flag meant or if they even had any concept of a truce, but it was the proper "Roman thing to do" when requesting a parlay.

It was important for the romans that the savages learned their ways, she thought. For them, negotiation was a fundamental part of the war of conquest; it accounted for at least half of the empire's subjects. It would be ironic if the Atrebates denied Metella the opportunity to negotiate because they were too savage to know any better. The legion had lost too many *negotiari* (negotiators) in Briton because the savages didn't know their customs…or was it because they chose not to honor the Roman custom of surrender?

Metella was having the same thoughts. He was gambling their lives that the Atrebates would have heard about the battle with the Catuvellauni at Wolf's Glen, that they would want to talk, to engage in negotiation before fighting. He was also betting their lives that Xara would make a difference. Such efforts at negotiation, especially in the north, had been spectacularly unsuccessful in the past. He had seen the savages return many *negotiari* with their heads cut off, their intestines trailing behind, or with other gruesome mutilations.

Despite his elaborate preparation, despite Xara's promise to cooperate, he knew this attempt to negotiate was a gamble. The Atrebates were even more savage, more primitive than the Catuvellauni…and they had the strategic advantage of the forest, which made it impossible for the Romans to use the well-disciplined, mass formations that had worked so well in open ground. The *Praefectus Castrorum* (military advisor and third in command of the legion), Prefect Gaius Lepidi had even gone on record his opinion that one legion would not be enough to create a foothold in the north. This opinion, documented by the legion's scribe, was the action that finally convinced the *Legatus Legionis* (the legion's commander) Legate Senatorus Plecio, to let him try negotiation. Still, it was a huge risk.

The girl, Xara, he thought, was still the biggest question. Despite her promise after the ugly business with Princess Ailios and during the torture of the slave Vela, to cooperate, would she keep her word, or would she revert to her savage ways? His instinct had told him that he had pushed her as far as she was going to go; that there were no guarantees. His instinct was that she needed to develop her own rationale for cooperating. She needed to work it out that Rome was here to stay and that the Britons had no choice but to cooperate.

He had seen this work before with animals, especially horses, but never with a slave. Slaves, even Britons, had the free will to defy their training. There came a time when they either accepted the conditions of their captivity or they rejected them. No amount of added pain or intimidation could force them to make an immutable choice.

He looked down at Xara then back along the forest trail. It was small comfort to remember that the entire Second Legion waited just at the edge of the forest for them to return, and if they did not, or if they returned in pieces, the legion would avenge them.

Yes, small comfort...

He had made sure that Xara had seen the legion preparing for battle before they left. He wanted her to understand that if their negotiations failed, the Second legion along with all the other legions that Rome would send would annihilate the Atrebates Tribe just as they had annihilated the Catuvellauni.

Of course, this assumed that she cared what happened to the Atrebates, which was an enormous leap of faith. Most Britons hated the other tribes almost as much as they hated Romans. Still, Xara, a Taexali, had joined with the Catuvellauni and fought with them. He was hoping that this experience would give her some sense of affiliation with other Britons.

He looked down at her again running beside at the end of his tether, her long chestnut hair streaming out behind, her skin gleaming with sweat. She was an incredibly beautiful creature, he thought, shaped like a curvaceous woman but tall and hard, harder than any Roman lady or any slave. She had lived her early life in primitive circumstances, and it showed. Fucking her had been an incredible experience and he was looking forward to doing it again.

He remember the night Viper had delivered her to him in the *arcus-atrox* (metal bow). His cock had nearly burst out of his pants. Whipping her, fucking her, playing with her hard body all the next day had been one of the greatest pleasures he had ever had in the legion. Not that he had had many pleasures. He had joined as a *veles* (a skirmisher) when he was fourteen, more than twenty years ago. He was lucky to have survived; the *velites* were the first to encounter the enemy and the first to die.

He remembered how she had fought him that first night, how he needed to tie her hands behind her back and tie her ankles to the far ends of the *arcus-atrox* before he could get to her cunt. Even then she had snapped at him with her teeth like a wild animal. A slave gag had stopped that, but she still resisted with her vaginal muscles, closing them as tightly as she could to prevent his penetration. It was no use, in fact, it was marvelous to feel her cervix gripping his cock so tightly.

She had been resisting him so furiously that she ignored her own feelings of arousal. She had suddenly lost it and began to move like a minx in heat once he had created a fucking rhythm. The result was inevitable. The incredible orgasm they both experienced was a terrible surprise to her, a shock to her system. He had seen it in her eyes when her massive contractions finally stopped. They had fucked like rabbits after that…for a full day.

But not since…

He had other uses for her now—important, lifesaving uses. He could not risk his plan, his promise to the prefect by continuing to fuck her. There were always plenty of other slaves to fuck if he needed release. None of them, however, could squeeze him as hard as she had done or provide so much other stimulation, but she was now destined for other things.

Right now, he needed to...

A lone figure appeared about twenty yards down the path just as they rounded another bend, presumably he was one of the Atrebates who had been tracking them. The muscular man had a short knife in his belt, and he was leaning casually on a vicious war club with a metal blade of some kind embedded at the end. Marcus guessed from his age and his imperious bearing that this was Togodumnus, son of Verica and war leader of the Atrebates. This was what the *dux carnifex*, the legions chief torturer, had learned from the Catuvellauni prisoners he had interrogated. He had also learned the disturbing fact that the Atrebates had nearly twice as many warriors than the Catuvellauni. Their campaign against the Atrebates would be a long and bloody if he failed to negotiate a settlement.

Metella slowed his mount and stopped about five yards in front of the man. He held up his empty hand—the universal sign of peace. Togodumnus just stared at him curiously. Metella knew that if he gave the signal to attack, they would be dead in seconds. The woods on either side were alive now with the movement of dozens of approaching warriors.

The centurion pulled hard on Xara's tether drawing her to a position near his left leg. She stared at Togodumnus, wondering if he would kill her as a Roman collaborator. Yoanie was buck naked, clearly a peace offering, a gift, but she wore the Roman belts, a sign that she was cooperating. She had the sudden errant thought that she would miss Metella magic cock.

"We come in peace," Metella said in a slow calming voice, "…from Rome. I represent the Roman commander, *Legatus Legionis* Senatorus Plecio. He has ordered me to parley with the great Verica of the Atrebates tribe and with his son, Togodumnus.

"Do you accept our request for parlay?"

The man was silent for several seconds, when he spoke his voice had a deep resonance that echoed through the trees. He spoke a guttural version of the Celtic tongue that Xara roughly understood.

"I do not speak your fucking language, Roman, and even if I did, you have nothing of interest to say to me. The only things I am interested in are your fine horses and your wet-cunt slave. Give them up now and I promise to give you and your man an easy death. The belted whore at your side, whom we assume is a collaborator, we will cook for her treachery. Oppose us and I will roast you as well, slowly over our campfire."

There was some rustling in the trees and even a few guffaws at his brief declaration. Togodumnus smiled. He obviously enjoyed playing to the crowd. Xara had no doubt that he was serious—a war leader didn't say things he did not mean especially on a battlefield.

Metella, of course, didn't understand a single word the Atrebates chief had said, but the man's mocking tone was clear enough—he had no interest in talking. Xara stayed silent…what could she say?

"If we do not parlay," Metella said with laudable calm, "…if we do not reach an agreement, the Roman legion at the edge of the forest will join with other legions and they will destroy the Atrebates as they destroyed the Catuvellauni."

…And the Taexali, Xara thought.

"Not one of the Atrebates will survive their assault. It will be death or slavery for every man, woman, and child in your tribe. We will crucify some of those who oppose us as examples to the others. You know what a crucifixion is like…you have seen it.

"Is this what you want for your people? Is this what your father wants?

"Talk to us, Togodumnus, negotiate with us. Your tribe can remain free here in the forest with your own chief under Roman rule. Instead of annihilation, we offer you an alliance. Let us talk together; you can always kill us tomorrow."

Marcus jerked hard on Xara's tether then nearly lifted her off her feet.

"Translate, damn you, Xara," he hissed at her. "Or you will be sucking Atrebates cock tonight."

"What blather do you speak Roman?" Togodumnus shouted. "Get off your horses and bow to me and I promise you will avoid the flames."

He lifted his war club and half turned to the nearby trees. Marcus's hand went to the hilt of his sword. They would not take him alive.

"Pardon, Master," Xara shouted out loudly towards Togodumnus.

She had not intended to cooperate with the Romans, but the thought of them roasting over an Atrebates campfire motivated her to try. The Atrebates version of Celtic was not the same as the Taexali's or the Catuvellauni's, but it was close enough for her to speak and understand. Metella relaxed his grip on her leash, and she hurriedly took a step to the side, as far as the tether would allow.

"The Roman dog holding my leash asks for a meeting with your glorious father, Togodumnus, to beg for him to not fight them," she yelled. "The Romans are afraid of the Atrebates. Their army of pigs is no match for Atrebates warriors. They will need more legions than they have in all the world to defeat the Atrebates. To beg your consideration, they offer this lush Catuvellauni slave. They are many others just as attractive in pens at their camp."

Togodumnus turned back and lowered his club to the ground. He was clearly surprised that the Roman had brought a translator. The slave spoke their tongue, poorly, but understandably, and she appeared to speak the Roman tongue as well. He was again curious.

"Come forward, cunt, so I can see you," he ordered. "Are you with the Romans...one of their dogs?"

"I am nothing, a slave, Master, captured by the Romans during their battle with the Catuvellauni. The Roman learned that I could speak his language and forced me to journey with him into the Atrebates forest."

Togodumnus smiled. He seemed to find this amusing and interesting.

"If you can speak to them, tell the Roman to dismount and lay down his weapons. I know he can kill himself with his blade before we reach him. It will be a sign of trust if he throws down his weapons."

Xara looked up at Metella and spoke.

"He orders you to lay your weapons on the ground as a sign of peace, *Ignavus*, and meet him eye to eye. It is probably a trick, and he will roast you over his campfire once you are disarmed and dismounted, but you have no other option if you want to meet with him."

It was clear from her tone that Togodumnus order was not negotiable.

Marcus looked at the man then at Xara. He suddenly realized that he needed to trust her; this was what all his preparations had been about, learning to trust her. If she was deceiving him now, he will have failed and he would deserve death. He lifted the truce flag and planted it in the soft ground then he dismounted, signaling his adjutant to do the same. Once on the ground, he removed his *gladius* and the knife he had taken from Xara and lay them on the ground. Both Romans held up open hands to show that they were empty of all weapons.

Togodumnus shouted an order, and five of his men ran onto the trail. They took the horses, Yoanie, and the weapons then disappeared down the trail. Xara stood off to Metella's side—he still had her tether wrapped around his hand—and the adjutant stood behind him.

"I am Togodumnus, war chief of the Atrebates, son of Verica. Tell the Roman pig to follow me," he said to Xara; "…tell him that if he tries any treachery, he will immediately suffer the flames as promised. My father might be curious to speak with him before we put him on a spit. As for you, Roman-talking slave, I think I will fuck you in your tight ass tonight. Would you like that?"

"As you wish, Master," Xara answered then turned to Metella and spoke to him in Latin.

"This is Togodumnus, son of Verica. He orders you to follow him to the Atrebates village where he will introduce you formally to his father. He says if you try any Roman treachery, he and his men will kill you here."

Metella nodded. Despite the extreme danger of their current situation, the fact that Xara was actively translating as he had planned elated him. He suddenly realized that she was not just translating, but she was also mediating. He knew these ignorant savages; they would sooner kill you than talk to you. She had obviously said what the savage needed to hear to let them live, at least long enough to begin the conversation with the Atrebates chief. This was the key to successful negotiation--take one small step at a time. Xara seemed to know this instinctively.

***

The Atrebates chief's residence was a large hut built around a central fire pit. Thick poles and beams placed throughout the structure supported its thatched roof. Togodumnus had had the female slave, Yoanie, suspended from one of the overhead beams by her wrists like a piece of meat, her long toes just barely touching thc ground. A large boar, skinned for roasting, hung from the same beam. It was clear from the identical way in which the slave and the boar were hung that the men inside the hut gathered around the fire considered them of similar value.

"I am Centurion Marcus Metella of the Second Roman Legion. This is Xara, a Taexali girl and my slave, whom I use as a translator. Our commander, *Legatus Legionis* Senatorus Plecio, has sent me here to discuss peace between the romans and the Atrebates.

"My commander would be honored if the great Verica, chief of the Atrebates, would accept this Catuvellauni woman as our gift, as a sign of our respect for him and his people." He pointed towards Yoanie. "She is one of the most desirable females we captured during the recent battle at Wolf's Glen when we defeated the Catuvellauni chief Caratacus.

We offer her to you as a gift, as a gesture of the good will the Roman emperor has for the Atrebates people."

Xara translated what he said exactly. She was curious about what the Roman expected to achieve with these Atrebates.

Metella wanted to insert Wolf's Glen into the conversation early. The Atrebates had certainly heard by now that the Romans had defeated the Catuvellauni tribe. This fact, more than any other argument, established their credentials.

The old man turned and said something to his son who stood and walked to the hanging slave. Yoanie great mane of flowing hair framed her face. Metella knew that most Britons admired a thick, healthy head of hair. The girl was clearly suffering from the suspension as she tried to balance herself on her toes.

Togodumnus smiled at her pain, ran his hands over her nubile body, then inserted two fingers into her cunt. The girl gasped then jumped as he put a finger from his other hand into her asshole. She writhed, trying to lift herself off his fingers, but it was impossible. He played with her, reaming her holes. Suddenly, he ended his buggering and snatched a rawhide knout (a knotted whip) from one of the posts and viciously applied it to her flailing legs. Everyone watched and waited while she screamed, kicking out wildly with her bare feet and legs. The men seemed comfortable with what was happening; they hut had obviously seen much pain. Togodumnus finished with the knout then turned and nodded to his father. He was clearly satisfied by the girl's response. He had been evaluating her sexual and pain response, just as he would evaluate a horse's strength and temperament.

Togodumnus returned to his place at the fire, washing and wiping his fingers with a smile of grudging acceptance on his face. Someone cut Yoanie down, collared with a rough strip of rawhide, and led away. Marcus was confident that she would be sucking on Togodumnus' balls tonight as a final test of her sexuality. Xara had sat stone-faced through the inspection, but Metella could see that the rough way Togodumnus had treated the girl bothered her; she had hoped that Yoanie would find a gentler master. Metella was concerned that she was bothered; he had assumed that she would remain neutral, unaffected by what was said.

"We accept the Roman Commander's gift," Verica said formally. "We are aware of the value that Romans place on such well-formed cunts and asses. We have heard that Romans even eat their food off the high asses of their whores."

Those around the old man laughed uproariously at his joke. Making fun of the Romans was clearly a favorite pastime in the hut.

"What did he say?" Metella asked Xara off to the side.

"The Chief accepts your gift with thanks," she answered with a straight face.

She knew she needed to be careful with both the Roman and with the Atrebates...they had the foolish pride of men, who were too often guided by their guts and their cocks. She didn't want to die because one of these men thought the other had slighted him.

"What was so funny about that?"

Xara shrugged. She had not thought that far ahead. Metella knew that there had been more to the exchange, but this was not the time to question the accuracy of the girl's translations. Togodumnus was now leering at her with obvious sexual interest.

"Rome wants peace with the Atrebates people," Metella started. "Towards this end, we ask that you agree to an alliance with the Roman Empire. This alliance has simple terms: you allow us to cross through the forest, through your land unhindered, and we will allow you to keep sovereign control over all that is now yours, free to govern those of your tribe without interference. Rome will also protect you from other tribes, aggressors who would challenge our agreement."

He waited until Xara had translated, which she did almost verbatim. This was the carrot, now for the stick.

"Protect...protect us? We need no fucking protection from Rome!" Togodumnus shouted.

Before Xara could translate, Metella spoke again, correctly interpreting the hostile tone of the war chief's reply.

"You understand, great Verica," he said, ignoring Togodumnus, that we cannot leave an enemy or a potential enemy at our rear. We know that the great chief and the great war chief of the Atrebates people will understand this basic principle of war and become our allies...our friends, protecting not threatening our backs."

Xara stared at him for a moment, shocked. She knew these people. She knew that they would be dead a few seconds after she translated such a blatant threat. This foolish centurion had no idea of how to deal with a proud Briton chief.

"Rome wants peace," she began slowly with her own version of what Metella had said. "Rome has heard of the great power of the Atrebates people, the wisdom and strength of its leaders. Rome wants to preserve its legions and will pay gold for peace and for the right to cross the Atrebates land. Rome has no desire to fight the great and powerful Atrebates tribe."

Verica nodded his head, clearly impressed with the mention of gold then he turned to converse quietly with Togodumnus and the other leaders of the tribe.

"How much?" he asked suddenly turning back towards the fire.

Xara turned to Metella.

"The Chief will consider your terms for an alliance, but he wants a tribute in gold to allow Roman soldiers to pass through the Atrebates forest."

"How much?" Marcus asked cautiously.

He had assumed that the lust for gold had not really taken root this far north and he was surprised by the request. He was also pleased that the chief had immediately turned towards avarice. They could work with such men. Xara turned back to Verica.

"The Roman says that they will pay the Atrebates your weight in gold each time a Roman legion passes through Atrebates land. With this amount of gold, the Atrebates chief can buy a hundred female slaves of breeding age at the slave depot in Rumabo."

Xara had no idea of the amount of gold needed to buy a hundred slaves, but she understood immediately that they needed to avoid abstractions with these simple men.

The chief nodded, impressed. He was a large man for a Brit.

"Tell him I want my weight and that of my son, Togodumnus."

She turned back to Metella.

"He wants his and his son's weight in gold each time a Roman legion passes through Atrebates land."

Marcus frowned then sat back as if considering the offer.

"Tell him that we will pay him his weight and that of his new slave girl in gold, as long as she remains slim and fit."

Xara translated exactly. The Roman was following her lead with the negotiation. The old chief nodded. Bargaining fairly and in good faith was a sign of respect. Metella nodded back. The deal was made.

Keeping a Roman legion intact to fight for more territory further north was worth ten times the amount the Chief had asked, he thought. Once they had a larger fighting force in the area, they could revisit the agreement he had struck with the Atrebates. Not only would the deal preserve the legion's men for more valuable treasure, but the Atrebates would be a source of much needed replacements.

Warriors from many of the tribes they conquered, and their tribal allies often joined the legions as auxiliaries. The more territory they conquered, therefore, the more ability they had to conquer even more territory. Everyone understood the importance of this force multiplier. Everyone also knew that an agreement was only valid if both parties needed the other.

"I accept on behalf of the Roman Empire," Metella said slowly, trying to look unhappy, as if the Chief had wrested more from him than he had expected.

Xara turned to Verica then turned back toward Metella.

"You should say more, Roman" she whispered. "He will expect you to thank him for his wisdom and to promise more gifts over time."

"Mind your own fucking business, slave," the centurion said with a smile. "Just tell him that I accept."

Xara turned back to the Chief.

"The Roman pig thanks the great Verica for his generosity and promises more gold and more slaves over time as their return from plundering the tribes to the north is substantial."

Verica rose smiling and faced Marcus who also stood up.

"Tonight, I will send you a luscious Atrebates slave for your bed, Roman. Try not to eat off her high ass."

There was more uproarious laughter from his entourage.

Xara paused for a moment then spoke directly to Metella with a serious expression on her face. She had had enough of Metella's manipulation.

"The chief is giving you one of his daughters to bed tonight, *Ignavus* This act will seal the agreement you've just made," she lied. "It is the custom of the Atrebates tribe that you should kiss her asshole when she is naked and bent over. It is a sign of great respect towards him and his tribe."

Metella smiled at the chief then stared hard at Xara.

"That's a very strange custom…"

Xara shrugged. After a time, Metella nodded accepting his gift.

He knew that all of Xara's translations had been "loose." It was disconcerting to not be able to know what she was saying, to be this dependent on the fucking promise of a slave. Their lives and the lives of the legion were in her hands.

He had already decided to punish her for her insolence in the translation process, but he had no idea of what she had said to the Atrebates. If she was going to continue as translator, he needed to have much more confidence in what she was saying. She could be valuable, just as he'd predicted, but he needed to keep her on a much tighter rein. There was no telling what she was telling these savages.

Still, because of his idea and his faith in her ability, the legion would pass through the Atrebates land without the loss of a single legionary. All that was necessary was a little talk, a little gold, and for him to kiss some Atrebates royal asshole. Not much, he though, considering…

Chapter Two - Retribution

“Do you think I'm stupid?” Metella growled, his face inches from hers. “Do you think that you can change my words, that you can say whatever *you* think is right to these savages?”

His rage was leaving white flecks on his lips.

“You are a fucking slave, Xara, the property of the Second Legion. I am your master. Do you understand what this means? Do you understand that I decide whether you eat or not, whether you go naked or not, whether you suffer or not?” I control everything that happens to you…good and bad. And it doesn’t matter if I fuck you every day.” He paused his diatribe and lifted the *ferula*. “Now I will punish you for your insolence.”

He struck her bare ass with the short slave whip, which was designed to inflict a viciously sharp pain with little effort but leave no mark. Xara yelped and her body jerked violently away from the pain then snapped back. She cursed her weakness, her inability to accept the roman’s pain without flinching like a little girl.

Viper, Sergeant Spurius Vipsanius, on the centurion’s orders had gleefully tied her in the usual position—between the two posts with her arms and legs spread and her feet off the ground—as soon as they returned from Verica’s camp. Viper disliked Xara; he resented the special “arrangement” she had with the centurion; he disliked the way she behaved—it was not normal for a slave—and he thought it reflected badly on him in the men's eyes. He was ecstatic whenever Metella ordered her bound for punishment.

Xara stared at him then glanced at the terrible lashes of the *ferula* dangle dangling from Metella's hand. She was frightened…of the pain, but not enough to admit that she had done anything wrong—she would take her sensible translations with her to the grave if necessary—but the more she denied any wrongdoing the angrier Metella got. He walked away, trying to calm himself.

"I hope he flays the skin off your ass," Viper whispered as he checked the ties on her wrists and ankles. "He is pissed enough to do it today. What did you do to him anyway during your stroll through the forest? We don't need uppity slaves like you around here…bad for morale."

She had been hoping that Metella would have ordered him to tie only her wrists for the whipping—she had seen them do that many times to others—but once again he had spread her legs and tied her ankles to the posts. Spread open like this, she lost its ability to twist, which doubled the pain.

"Be careful about pissing him off too badly," Viper warned sarcastically as he squeezed one of her nipples. "If you end up in my hands, you will wish you'd never been born."

Xara waited until his face was close enough then she spit in his eye. His hand reached for his gladius then stopped. The centurion would crucify him if he killed her, his special slave.

“I don't need to end up in your hands to wish I were dead, snake-man,” she hissed so only he could hear. “The smell of you is bad enough so that I already wish that.”

He stared at her with a fierce hatred then he adjusted the four ropes to stretch her body to its ultimate limit, which would increase the *ferula's* pain even more. Her tight skin literally crawled as she thought about the whip strokes to come, about the way they she would burn. Viper stepped as Metella approached. She could see the sergeant fighting to suppress his instinct to murder her. It was only his fear of pain and death that saved her from him gutting her. Despite her fear, she smiled to further enrage him.

He stepped back to her side and whispered in her ear so Metella could not hear.

“One day, cunt, one day he will deliver you to me. When that happens, I will make you suffer like no one has ever suffered. Remember this.”

Xara hated all romans, but viper held a special place in her heart. To her, he was the living symbol of everything that was evil about Rome and Romans. She hated Metella as well, but Metella truly believed in Rome's civilizing effect, in the benefits of a *pax Romana* for Briton; he thought his negotiations would save lives, but Viper…Viper, a weak man at heart, enjoyed the opportunity to dominate; he took great satisfaction even pleasure in making people suffer. For him, there was nothing noble or purposeful in the carnage Rome wrought, there was not even a sexual or emotional aspect to it, he just enjoyed bringing pain and misfortune to others.

"And if the Gods put you in my hands," Xara whispered in reply, "you can expect the same."

She had heard his quick intake of breath and was satisfied. For all his evil, Viper was the real coward, not Metella. She called him *ignavus* to express her ongoing resistance to her enslavement.

The centurion took his position again and putt half-a-dozen strokes down her back. He stepped back from her writhing body and watched her long muscles ripple with the pain. There was no hiding the *ferula's* effect. Everything about her was tight and lean like a dog in perfect condition, one exercised for speed and strength.

The salve was incredibly desirable when she suffered, Metella decided. Her long torso and shapely legs, the pointed firmness of her breasts, the hardness of her ass all taunted him with their suffering; they distracted him from his righteous purpose. He should not be fucking her, he thought; he had convinced himself it was part of her punishment, her domination, but that was a lie. He enjoyed her hard body, enjoyed the way she moved in his arms, the way she came…with the wild abandon of an animal rather than a refined Roman lady. In a way, she had bewitched him, addicted him to her fucking.

Thinking about Xara, about her hard ass and swollen cunt reminded him of the Atrebates chief's daughter. He was nearly one-hundred percent sure now that Xara had tricked him into kissing her ass.

The girl had been surprised when he had bent her over respectfully, carefully spead her ass cheeks wide, and kissed her asshole. She had even giggled as if *he* were the butt of some perverse joke. That was the moment when he realized that Xara had tricked him. There was no Atrebates' custom of kissing theroyal daughter's asshole. She had made a fool out of him!

"Was she even royal?" he screamed. "Was she even the king's daughter?"

Xara turned her sweat covered face towards him and smiled infuriatingly through her pain.

"She was a whore, *Ignavus*, a slave, a tight piece of ass. It is their custom to offer a girl to emissaries, but you were the first one to kiss the whore's ass.... The whole tribe was laughing about it the next day. They now think it's a roman custom."

Metella, now fully enraged, laid the tip of the whip hard across her tits and nipples, alternating from one side to the other. The stroping sound of the leather on bare skin echoed in the night. Xara threw back her head and screamed; she was trying to control her reactions, but the pain was cutting into her brain like a hot knife.

He stepped back breathing heavily. This fucking cunt has made Rome the butt of savages' jokes; she has made a fool out of me, he thought...*A FOOL!* Was the demand for tribute even real; had it come from Verica or from her? He pulled back his arm and struck her between the legs over and over until they were cherry red. She was panting and trembling from head to toes, pulling desperately on the four straps that bound her to the posts when he finally stopped. Viper, watching from a distance smiled.

"This is going to be one whipping you will never forget, Xara. *NEVER!*"

He moved to her back and oput his hand between her legs to feel the heat of the whipstrokes. She was staring at him, still glaring at him with wild intensity as she tried to catch her breath.

"Why did you let me think that girl the chief's daughter?" he demanded. "Why did you trick me into kissing her ass?"

"Ro...Ro...Romans are only fit to kiss the asses of whore, *Ignavus*," Xara hissed. "It is a fitting act for jackals."

Her smokey eyes were now wide open and definant. Even as she anticipated the agony of his next round of whip strokes, she was in rebellion...and still calling him "Ignavus" with the same disgust. It was incredibly stupid, perhaps also brave, to do that during normal times, but it was insane to do it spread open between two posts and under torture. Even though she had agreed to translate, her defiance was still there, hidden, still lurking behind a wafer-thin shell of self-preservation.

If he didn't need her so badly, he thought, he would crucify her as an example to the others.

"Do you want me to crucify you?" he asked, frustrated. "You have seen what it is like to die on the cross, is this what you want?"

He wanted he to comply, to see the value of what he was trying to do, to fuck him because she wanted him, not because he tied her to the cot. They had urgent matters to attend to, thousands of lives, Roman and Briton, depended on them. Why couldn't she see through her hatred and...

"Did the Atrebates girl fuck you like a royal, *Ignavis*?" Xara asked softly, her face down, "or like a..." she hesitated, "like a slave...like you require me to do?"

Metella took a step back, enraged that she was still mocking him. He reached for a wooden paddle. He had not intended to use the terrible implement on her but her behavior was intollerable. He move behind and used the paddle to stike her ass with increasing force. Each stroke on her already-raw skin brought a full-throated scream from her throat. She had never experienced such agony. He stopped just short of raising blood then stood back. The gutteral sounds coming from her mouth attested to her condition.

"Now just tell me straight," he screamed into her face, "why did you do it? Can I still trust you or should I just end this now and put you on the cross?"

Viper smiled even more broadly. Xara raised her head. Drool was flowing from her mouth and her face was dripping sweat.

"Yes, *Ignavus*," she hissed through clenched teeth. "Yes, my fucking Roman master!" She screamed. "You can trust me to do what I said I would do. I do not break my work like Romans do, but I will not translate a message that will accomplish nothing and just get us killed. It's not just the words you speak, Roman, it's your fucking arrogance. You need more than translation..."

She stopped and stretched her lithe body like a cat.

"The girl was a whore, *Ignavus*, but giving her to you was a gesture of respect by the Atrebates chief. He heard *my* words and gave you a whore for your pleasure!"

Metella watched her face for signs of treachery. Could she be telling the truth? Had she changed his words so that they could succeed with their mission? Was she right that her judgement was better than his with these people? There was no way to know the answers. More importantly, the truth was unimportant, all that was important was the result—they had a treaty with the Atrebates; the legions could pass through the forests unimpeded.

He suddenly backed away from the girl's trembling body and poured himself a cup of wine. Could he trust her? He had convinced the prefect and the legate that using Xara as a translator would allow them to achieve inexpensive victories with the Britons through negotiation rather than through battle, which could save hundreds if not thousands of lives. And it had worked with the Atrebates—they had met with Verica and Togodumnus, the tribe's war leader, and they had worked out a deal. Or had they? The chief had given him a girl to fuck who Xara, in her translation, told him was the chief's daughter. Now she was telling him she was the tribe's whore, but that it was still a mark of respect. What else had she lied about? Did it matter?

"D... Did... Did you really kiss her ass, *Ignavus*?" Xara asked innocently.

The waves of recurring pain from his paddling were still making it difficult for her to speak.

"Did you bury your face deeply between the whore's ass cheeks and ream out her asshole? I hope she could feel your tongue in her."

Metella studied Xara's tortured face. Was she telling the truth about changing his words for their greater purpose or did she trick me? The personal insult doesn't matter, he concluded, in light of the strategic importance of the treaty. Even if she did insult him, she has been punished for it.

"Fuck with me like that again slave and I will nail you to the fucking stockade wall," he hissed into her face, angry beyond words. "You will beg me for death. BEG ME...! Do you understand, cunt?"

"Beg you for death, Ignavus?" Xara answered him calmly, undaunted by the threat. "I would never beg you for death as long as I can still think, as long as I can still remember my family, my people, as long as I can see the images of all the innocent people Rome has enslaved and tortured, killed for no reason other than conquest. I will keep my promise," she hissed, "but not because I fear your toture or death, *Ignavus*, but because the work of a Taexali is valuable."

Was she mocking him yet again? Was she spitting in his face with clever words? Was she really loyal to her promise, if so why? Suddenly, he knew that he would never have the truth from her. This hellion would take her secrets with her to her grave. He should have known that someone this intelligent, this savage was not going to capitulate to a whip or a paddle. The first moment they had met, she had invited crucifixion by kicking him. There was no limit to how far a savage mind like hers would go for revenge.

"Are the Atrebates committed to the agreement we discussed? Xara," he asked menacingly. "Careful how you answer this question, cunt; fucking with me personally is dangerous enough, but putting the legion in harm's way is deadly."

"Are the Atrebates committed to the agreement we have agreed?" he asked again.

Xara stared at him as beads of sweat ran down her face and arms. Her mouth was open, and she was breathing heavily from the paddle's pain.

"Yes, *Ignavus*. They are committed. Just deliver the gold to them and they will allow the legion to pass through the forest unharmed," she answered coolly.

Sweat continued to roll off her bare shoulders and drip off the ends of her nipples as he studied her eyes. He knew she was in agony but determined not to show it in front of him. Suddenly he realized something else—there was no way to confirm the truth of anything she said."

This was a dilemma he had not anticipated. She was the only one who could speak Latin and the Celtic language of the Atrebates. They had to trust her…he had to trust her. If he expressed any uncertainty about the agreement to the legate or to his mentor and friend, the prefect, Gaius Lepidi, he would look like a fool. Even more important, they would look like fools for supporting his idea of negotiation. He could not let this happen; he could not let them down. As much as he had doubts, he had to let this play out. If he was going to use this bitch, he needed to trust her...

"Do you think I would risk a Roman legion on your word alone, Xara? I need proof that you speak the truth."

"Proof..." she looked at him with all the scorn her tortured body could muster.

"A great Roman soldier, a leader such as you is unsure of the truth...so unsure that he needs proof...from his cunt slave?" Her voice was rising in anger at each word. "My invincible, infallible Roman *master* is unsure of something? He needs his *slave* to assure him of the truth."

Metella took a step back. The rage in her eyes hovered on insanity. Rage had corded the muscles in her bound arms and legs. He was suddenly afraid that in her madness she would actually break bones.

"You are the slave here, Xara," he shot back. "I am the master. Remember this. It is the reality of our situation. Dying on the cross is slow and painful as you know. It is a death fit only for murderers and traitors. Is this what you want? Do you want revenge on us so badly that you are willing to die for it on a Roman cross? I can arrange that. In five minutes, I can have you nailed to the wood and hanging with your feet swinging in the air. Viper would view such an order as a reward. Is that what you want?"

"You would have me nailed to your roman wood, *Ignavus*? Isn't nailing the quicker and therefore the kinder method of death? Why not have me strapped as you did with the *Catuvellauni* women you tortured and killed? You speak of revenge... My revenge is nothing compared to the atrocities you will commit as a Roman in the fucking line of duty. Be a man, *Ignavus*! Admit your own wrongdoing."

He reeled back from her verbal assault.

"You have no fucking idea what you are doing, *Ignavus*, with these negotiations," she whispered viciously. "If I had said your words to the Atrebates chief, we would both be roasting over an Atrebates fire. Yes, I changed your fucking Roman words, but I did not change their intent. And yes, the Atrebates chief did agree with your basic proposal, but only after I sucked his cock with my slave words."

Metella studied her eyes. There was still rage in them but no deceit.

"The idea that Rome should pay gold, however," she spat out victoriously, "was mine not the Chief's. Take your fucking legion north without fear, *Ignavus*. They will be safe, at least through the Atrebates forest. Or, if you are too fearful of the words spoken by your whipped slave then cower here behind your camp's pointed walls. It makes no fucking difference to me."

Her words struck Metella dumb. They implied that the Atrebates might *not* have agreed to allow the Legion to pass. He had already given Gaius his report of a successful negotiation and Gaius had passed it on to the legate. All six thousand of the legion's men were preparing to move out through the forest based on *his* negotiated settlement. The commander had already sent him a congratulatory scroll for a job well done.

This was a disaster. He would look like a complete idiot in front of everyone if he cast suspicion on the negotiations, his negotiation now. It would mean the end of his career, maybe the end of his life. The legate, Senatorus Plecio, was not a forgiving man, neither was Gaius. He remembered the prefect's last words to him: "Whatever you do, don't embarrass me."

Impossible! It was impossible for him to back away from his report now. He turned back to the naked girl.

"You bitch! You will walk behind my horse on a leash as we pass through the Atrebates land. If there is any hint of treachery, I will carefully slit you open from cunt to throat and let my dogs feast on your guts." He was livid with renewed rage.

Xara stared at him without fear.

"Now...now we both understand why I call you *Ignavus*, Roman," she said softly.

"Who else but a fucking coward would risk the lives of thousands of his fellow Romans to avoid the shame of failure. You are even worse than an ordinary coward; you are a hypocrite as well, placing a higher value on your honor, your personal pride than on the lives of your men.

"Coward!" she repeated slowly. "Coward! Coward! COWARD!"

Metella suddenly saw red and used the paddle viciously on her flanks. He couldn't stop. Her behavior was outrageous, beyond his experience. She had bested him in this Atrebates affair, humiliated him, forced him to dishonor himself, caused him to put his friendship with the prefect at risk. Her suffering was nothing compared to the damage she had done.

He stopped when his arm grew tired then he sat back down on a stool and watched her writhe in well-earned agony for a full ten minutes. Her entire body was glowing red with welts from the paddle. As he watched her suffer, it slowly occurred to him that even though she had taken advantage of the situation, it was his ego and ambition that had caused the farce to come apart so badly.

"I am going to take you back to my tent and fuck you now, Xara," he said softly. "Fuck you as you scream with ongoing pain then I am going to laugh when you come. This will remind me that in the end, you are just another woman and a slave.

Xara stared at him without responding. She knew that him fucking her now would be further punishment, terrible punishment, but somehow it didn't matter. Incredibly, a part of her wanted him to do it.

***

It took almost six full days for the four-thousand eight-hundred and forty men of the Second Roman Legion to pass through the Great Northern Forest, through Atrebates territory. At the head of the column were *Legatus Legionis* Senatorus Plecio, *Tribunus Laticlavius* Artimus Concerti, his political adviser and second in command. Both of them rode high in their saddles, blissfully unaware of the danger that Metella had uncovered during Xara's interrogation.

The prefect, the legate's military advisor, *Praefectus Castrorum* Gaius Lepidi, rode far behind them near the first fighting cohort, his head swiveling from side to side searching for danger. He had detected a hint of doubt in Metella' eyes and, without saying anything, at the last minute, had turned down the legate's invitation to ride triumphantly at the front of the legion. Lepidi told him that out of an abundance of caution he would remain with the first cohort "just in case the savages have any treachery in mind."

"Just another precaution," Prefect Gaius had repeated to the legate, but his eyes were like steel. He knew that Metella was holding something back about the negotiations and he was greatly worried and annoyed. But the centurion remained stubbornly silent about any misgivings he might have.

The prefect had also ordered Metella to ride at the head of the Second Cohort of 480 men including the legion's one-hundred and twenty cavalrymen in support of the legion's front and back. The legate had already promoted him to Senior Centurion for his good work in successfully negotiating with the Atrebates and given him command of the prestigious First Cohort as a reward.

As he had promised, Metella had Xara walk just behind his horse on a short leash wearing the same belt harness he had used during the ride to the negotiation. The belts signaled her elevated status to the men, but Metella still suspected treachery.

He had ordered that both of his *canes pugnaces* (war dogs) receive no food for three days. The large and heavy animals ran alongside her, confused by the punishment. They had light brown eyes, truncated muzzles, broad muscular backs, and legs that seemed particularly well-suited to holding a victim in place while they ripped out its throat. Xara thought about this as they ran at her side. Metella had bred and trained the dogs to be a merciless killer, but they had always been surprisingly gentle around Xara. That would change if Metella carried out his threat to eviscerate her and have the two mastiffs devoured her alive at the first sign of trouble. Xara appeared unbothered by the promise and even stayed close to the animal, but she was concerned that her life was in the fickle hands of Verica and his even more volatile son, Togodumnus.

But their fears were unfounded, there was no trouble from the tribe. The legion passed through the forest without incident. When the legion reached the river as Chief Atrebates and War Chief Togodumnus were standing peacefully on the bank, watching. On one side of them was the Roman tribute wagon filled with the gold Xara had added to the negotiation, on the other side was the slave girl Yoanie collared and chained to a second beautiful slave. As they got closer, Metella could see that the second slave girl was the one the chief had given him to fuck the night of the negotiation, the one whose asshole he had kissed, the one he thought was a princess, the chief's daughter.

Metella looked back at Xara, who was moving along at a steady pace set more by the infantry column behind than by his Metella's horse. She looked up innocently. Metella turned back to the front just as Togodumnus pursed his lips and mimed a kiss. The centurion didn't respond to the taunt as he passed, although his face was a bright red under his helmet. The chief's was giggling like a child, and the normally taciturn Verica was struggling to hold back a smile.

Even though both parties were honoring the agreement, Metella knew that their amusement was proof that Xara had tricked and humiliated him. He vowed to make her suffer even more than he already had; he would fuck her until she begged him for mercy, until she…

An officer approached on horseback from the front of the column and Metella put aside his thoughts of vengeance. He nodded as the man turned his horse smartly to ride at his side. It was the equestrian tribune, the legion's young representative of the patrician class, *Tribune Augusticlavii* Atticus Versus. He was from a wealthy family serving his time in the legion as one of the legate's adjutants.

"The *legatus legionis* sends his complements and congratulations, Centurion," he said officiously. "Your negotiations appear to have truly saved us from a bloody fight. Of course, they also denied the legion another glorious victory, but there will be more opportunities further north, I'm sure, eh?"

Metella nodded but retained his stonily silence. The tribune was an ass, as most patricians were, but he was still young. The assignment to a front-line legion like the Second might change him.

"In any case, this is a great and wonderous day. We are the first legion to cross the Great Norther Forest and the first to travel this far north. The *legatus legionis* expects that we will conquer rich lands for Rome and take many slaves, some for ourselves, eh, thanks to you."

Metella nodded again. After the taunt from Togodumnus, talking to the rich-boy junior officer was the last thing he wanted to do. Even on his best days, he was generally uncomfortable with the legion's politics and its political appointees.

"The *legatus legionis* asks that you join him for supper tonight to celebrate," the tribune said with the imperious air of an emperor. "He wants to discuss further ways in which your amazing slave and your superb negotiating skill might be of use to the legion."

Metella smiled and nodded his agreement. There was no other possible response. If only these people knew how close they had been to total fucking disaster; how Xara, the naked slave girl running behind at the end of his tether, had negotiated their fate with the Atrebates' leader not him.

"He asks that you bring your amazing slave. He and the other tribunes are burning with curiosity about her. You might want to cloth her though...for the *legatus legionis's* sake," Atticus advised. "Such a shame," he joked, "a body like that, even on a savage, should never be hidden. She is a magnificent creature, no?"

Atticus wet his lips and glanced back at the girl leaving little doubt of what was on his mind.

"She will probably be reassigned to a more experienced negotiator, one closer to the *legatus legionis*, one who knows intimately the strategic goals for the legion in this region," he said in an offhand manner. "I'm sure that a soldier like you would welcome the release from the political duties of a negotiator, eh? You created her, but now especially as the legion's *primus pilus* (senior centurion) you must have many more important things to attend to, eh?"

Metella was sure that the legate or his political advisor had sent Tribune Atticus Versus to give him advance warning that they were assigning Xara to a "more experienced negotiator." The prefect would not want his protégé blindsided. The man waited for a reply, but Metella wasn't sure how he felt.

Receiving no response, he nodded, took a final leering glance at Xara, and spurred his horse to a flawless gallop.

Metella watched him ride off. This is good, he thought, I'll finally be rid of the infuriating bitch. The legate, his number two, and all their fucking minions can deal with her treachery themselves. The legion didn't pay him enough to screw around with such a complicated creature. Of course, he would miss fucking her, but in war, it was necessary to make sacrifices.

He glanced back at Xara. She was smiling up at him with a scornful expression. He ground his teeth, instantly understanding the reason for her smirk. She had jeopardized the legion; she had stolen hundreds of pounds of gold from Rome's coffers; she had tricked him into kissing a slave girl's asshole; and she had made him a figure of ridicule to a bunch of savages…all while under his domination.

He thought about the serious damage she could do as translator for one of the legate's minions then shrugged. There was nothing he could do to prevent it without revealing her duplicity and his own failing in the Atrebates affair.

He had created a monster in the guise of a beautiful slave.

***

"Have her strip for us, Centurion," the boy, Tribune Atticus Versus, yelled drunkenly across the table. “She is quite a gorgeous specimen. I'm sure the legate wants to have the total picture.”

His drunken comment was a terrible gaff at a legate dinner, but the young tribune was drunk, and no one said anything. There were five of them at the table—the legate, his number two, *Tribune Laticlavius* Artimus Concerti, the young tribune Atticus Versus, under the legate’s protection and acting as his adjutant, Prefect Gaius Lepidi, and him, Centurion Marcus Metella.

Xara knelt collared and chained at the centurion’s feet like a well-trained dog. He had followed the tribune's advice and dressed her in a brief white tunic that extended from just above the crest of her breasts to just below her ass. He had also put the girl in a collar and leash, hoping to deflect the rumor that she was too much for him to handle. Giving her over to someone else was one thing; doing it under a cloud of weakness was quite another.

Metella glanced up at the legate. He wanted to get this over with as quickly as possible, to be rid of her at the earliest moment, but he didn't understand the protocol of the command tent. Gaius, who sensed his discomfort, spoke for him.

“She speaks Latin, Legate,” he said. “Perhaps this is a good opportunity to see how well she responds to the person you intend to designate as the legion’s official negotiator.”

The legate had announced earlier that evening that he was placing her and taking the responsibility for future negotiations from the prefect’s military domain and placing it under an officer in his political contingent, but he didn't say who. The legate enjoyed the suspense, the mystery.

"Thank you, Prefect. I have appointed the *tribune laticlavis*, Artimus Concerti, my number two, to act as the legion's negotiator." He turned to Metella. "This is nothing against you, Centurion, I just feel that negotiations are better done by somewhat schooled in the art of politics rather than a military man."

"Of course, Legate," Metella answered.

Xara didn't respond to the announcement. Metella had warned her of what was happening beforehand.

"However, I do think that my young friend's suggestion that we allow Tribute Concerti to take charge of his new slave is appropriate."

Concerti stood up and nodded uncertainly. He was also a bit drunk.

"Excellent idea, Sir. I would like to see how she responds as well."

"Stand up girl and remove your tunic," Concerti ordered. "My friends and I want to see how well you are formed."

Xara looked up at Metella then rose to her feet and obediently slipped the tunic over her head in one smooth motion. She stood naked in front of the men, unashamedly pushing out her breasts and pubic mound in the tribune's direction. There was a silent intake of breath from everyone at the table. The girl was incredibly beautiful.

"How is it you know our tongue and our ways so well?" Concerti asked as he took his seat.

"I was held at a slave camp as a Roman prisoner for several months, Master, 'to ripen' they said. That was what the slave master told me. He thought I would bring a better price on the block if I was more mature."

Concerti nodded at the other men impressed with her response and her nuanced command of the language. It was common in the slave camps to set aside certain well-formed slaves for further growth. Xara was certainly beautiful enough to bring a premium price with the right preparations and the right grooming.

"How did you come to be among the Catuvellauni?"

"I escaped and they helped me evade the slave hunters, Master," she said, trying to stick as closely as possible to the truth.

She had no intention of admitting to this group that she had escaped from the slave depot at Rumabo Imperium after killing the Ninth Legion's commander, who had been trying to rape her.

The tribune nodded again apparently pleased with her direct answers.

"After your success with the Atrebates, the legion will want to use you again as a translator," Concerti declared, "but not under the centurion's direction. As you know, he is a fighting man not a politician. The legate has decided that you can serve us better under my leadership." The tribune turned towards the commander and nodded. "Our glorious leader has also named me as the legion's chief negotiator."

The legate smiled and nodded, confirming his decision. Metella felt sick at the undisguised ass-kissing.

Concerti pointed at the legate. "Go to His Honor's side," he ordered the girl.

The tribune turned towards the commander to comment on the girl's looks, but the legate's eyes were still on Xara who stood motionless in the center of the tent.

"I said kneel over here beside the legate," concerti repeated, annoyed at having to give the order twice in front of the other men.

The girl didn't move, she just stood there naked with her head bowed. All the men were staring at her now which was exactly what she wanted.

"May I speak, Commander?" she asked in a trembling voice, speaking directly to the legate, and ignoring both the tribune and the centurion.

Metella stared at her with disbelief. Xara simply didn't know fear. She had attacked a line of Roman legionaries with a knife, naked and painted blue; she had struck a Roman officer while in chains; she had fermented a slave rebellion; engineered the impaling of a royal Princess; and made him a fool in front of the Atrebates. Now she was defying a tribune and speaking with a *legatus legionis* as if she was his equal.

"Go ahead," the legate said with an amused voice.

"I do not know the tribune," she offered in an uncharacteristically gently tone; however, the wild Britons only respect war skills and courage in battle. The centurion stands as a warrior before them—everything he says and does mark him as such—and the chiefs of the northern tribes will respond to him for this reason."

She turned to Concerti who seemed confused.

"With respect, sir, they will not have the respond in the same way to a tribute who is, in the final analysis, a great statesman but not a soldier."

The legate blinked and shook his head as if he had just seen magic performed—a naked slave girl, a savage, standing in his tent was conversing with them, presuming to give him advice on how to conduct his campaign. He leaned back and considered the most appropriate death for such behavior. Metella also stared open-mouthed. He had just assumed that Xara would go meekly to the tribune under the assumption that she could manipulate him more easily. Her words even struck the prefect dumb. The unflappable engineer of a hundred glorious victories was at a loss for words. She had shocked all of them into silence.

It was the prefect, however, who recovered first. As expected, his first instinct was to protect his protégé, Metella.

"The cunt has a good point, Commander," he said. "These Brit savages are not ready for statecraft; they are barely out of the caves. Trying to approach them with the sophisticated negotiations that Tribune Concerti would offer might be premature. The savages might not receive or understand the tribute as well as a soldier."

The political instincts of Tribune Concerti also rallied at the General's left-handed complement.

"Yes, this girl might have a point, Prefect, but I think I can be trusted to gauge the level of discussion necessary to win over a simple Briton," he retorted.

"Of course, Tribune," Gaius answered quickly. "I was not implying otherwise, but what if they are unable to comprehend your sophisticated message? Do we really want them to slow-cook one of our senior commanders, a tribune from a glorious Roman family, over a Brit fire? What kind of a message would that send to the other tribes...or to Rome? A centurion on the other hand...," he turned and smiled generously at Metella, "...even one as valuable as the new *primus pilus* is expendable. The legion would greatly miss his talents of course but we would recover. Losing a tribune from a great Roman family on the other hand would give an enormous political victory to his killers, perhaps more than we can afford to have an adversary acquire especially this far north."

The tent was quiet awaiting the legate's verdict on the debate. Finally, he spoke.

"You're right as usual, Prefect," he said thoughtfully. "A tribune, even one as capable as Artimus Concerti, cannot be placed in such mortal danger. We need to use his skills sparingly for more important political duties. Governing these conquered people for the centuries to come is the real goal here not massacring them."

He turned to Metella.

"I'm afraid, Centurion, that the prefect is right. You will need to remain our field negotiator for a while longer. Are you still willing?"

The question was rhetorical. No one ever said they were unwilling to follow the legate's suggestions. Metella stood and saluted formally. Out of the corner of his eye he saw Xara slowly close one eye to wink at him. Not only had she outmaneuvered him, but she had now manipulated the commander of a Roman legion and his senior staff.

"...And use your whip more sparingly, Centurion," the legate added noting the red marks still visible on the girl's bare ass and legs. "This slave is a valuable asset of the Second Legion. I don't want her punished unnecessarily, and, of course, you should refrain totally from having sexual relations with her. As I said, she is important to our ultimate victory over the savages."

Metella reddened then saluted again and walked out, holding her tunic in one hand and leading the naked Xara by her collar chain. Her head was respectfully bowed, but there was a small smile on her face visible only to Metella.

Which of us are the masters here and which are the slaves, he wondered?

Chapter Three - The Picts

The vast and flowing grasslands absorbed the sound of Viper's whip and shrieks of the gift slave. As usual, Xara took her strokes without making any noise, but the other two girls were screamers. They were in Pict land now. Metella had ordered his sergeant to be especially strict with the three slaves. Always careful to follow such orders to the letter, viper kept up a steady barrage of stokes on their bare backs.

In truth, the gift slaves was exaggerating the whip's effect. They were in excellent shape and even though they were both naked and wrist-bound to the centurion's saddle pommel, they had no trouble keeping pace with his slowly moving horse. Nor did Viper, following behind, have any good reason to keep reaching down with his whip other than a predisposition towards cruelty. The centurion's indifferent order was just a license for him to exercise his sadistic impulses.

Metella looked back and watched their naked bodies move. Like many Brit women, the gift-slaves he had selected from the horse pen had good figures—long legs, firm tits, high asses. They were a gift for the Pict chief, Tininor. Beautiful young girls, slaves who made a man's blood hot, were a common gift from a tribe seeking favor from another. Metella only hoped he had made the right choice, that Tininor would find these two…arousing. Xara ran behind on a tether as well, still dressed in her three belts. She stayed close to the dogs, however, maintaining a respectable distance from Viper and his whip.

Viper had been even more morose than usual during their ride, stirring only to swing his whip into the ass or legs of one of his naked charges. He had been surprised when the centurion had ordered him along on the mission. His job of late had not been to fight like an ordinary soldier, but rather to administer discipline and oversee interrogations for the centurion. He, for example, had crucified the seven Catuvellauni women the centurion had used to convince Xara to cooperate and to break the hold Princess Ailios had on the prisoners.

Risking him and his torture and execution skills on such a stupid mission as this one to the Picts was an outrageous overreach of the Centurion's authority...in his view. He had been stewing about it for hours as they rode, thinking about how he would get a scribe to write an official complaint to the prefect when they returned. Perhaps one of the tribune's scribes would help him...they had become "familiar" over the last few weeks, ever since the centurion's dinner with the legate.

"When do we make contact with the savages, Centurion?" Viper asked in a tense voice. "These grassy hills probably go on for another hundred miles. What if we have missed them?"

"They have been tracking us for hours," Metella answered calmly. "They will make contact when they are ready; and you are to remain absolutely silent and still when they do stop us,

Sergeant. Do you understand? I don't want anything to spook them."

"What about your special girl, Centurion? Can you trust her to stay quiet, to give us an honest translation?" Viper asked.

He had guessed that the reason the centurion had whipped his Brit translator so viciously after the negotiation with the Atrebates was because she had somehow disobeyed or betrayed him during those negotiations. He didn't know how she had done that exactly as the Atrebates seemed to be adhering to the treaty, but he knew something was amiss between them.

"You leave her to me, Sergeant," the centurion answered. "Just be sure you do as I say."

The Centurion had already turned in his saddle to face forward.

Viper struck one of the gift slaves for no reason other than to express his anger with her scream then he smiled at Metella's back. The great Centurion Marcus Metella was afraid of his own slave. It was obvious that since the incident with the Atrebates, whatever that was about, he did not trust her! Viper had long suspected that the girl would try to fuck them at some point. It was always the same with the fanatical savages. They were uncontrollable, better to put them down like a rabid dog then to trust them. Putting down a creature as luscious and as eminently fuckable as Xara would be hard, but it was the only way.

Now that Metella had his own doubts, perhaps he could convince him to give him the girl to kill.

Of course, he wouldn't do that immediately, he would torture and fuck her for a few days before dispatching her to the savage's afterlife. It would happen…eventually, he was sure of it. The centurion had boxed himself into a corner with her. He had overpromised his friend, the prefect, about what she could or would deliver. Metella had even presented her to the legion commander as their "alternative to battle." The centurion had trapped himself; she had fucked him! It would be different when she was in his hands…he would be the one doing the fucking not her.

He struck on of the slave girls again and she screamed. His aim with the horse whip was unerring; even with Xara the Taexali girl; the problem was she hardly ever screamed. He would get her to scream, all he needed was…

Viper smiled thinly at his own ambitions. He had guessed Xara's game long ago and he had little sympathy for the centurion, who he considered an overbearing self-righteous prick.

"Listen to me, Sergeant," Metella hissed, turning back in his saddle to face him again. "You are not loitering around the camp now abusing the slaves in the pens. Our actions here will determine our fate once we meet the Picts. I suggest you shut your fucking mouth and do what I tell you to do without question or hesitation. For now, just concentrate on keeping these slaves moving, nothing more."

"Yes, Centurion," Viper replied, with a tone just shy of disrespect.

As a rule, Viper never trusted any slave no matter how docile or obedient. Once a prisoner has tasted the whip, once you forced a man or a woman to kneel and kiss your feet, you could never trust them again. It was just human nature. No matter how subservient and obedient they appeared, they would always harbor a resentment and if given the chance, take revenge. Even the most abject coward among them would harbor thoughts of revenge and take it whenever possible.

The centurion was insane to entrust their lives to this Briton bitch. The only advanced though these savage Brits had was vengeance. They were not human; they were more animal than human. They lived waiting for the opportunity for payback, suffered the pains of Hell for it. He knew them much better than the centurion. He had seen the hate in their eyes up close as they suffered and died. They will kill us all if given half a chance.

They rode on, the silence occasionally punctuated by a girl's scream. Metella had ordered them gagged before they left the camp...a security precaution he'd said, but then ordered their gags removed. Security...why? Viper preferred to keep slaves always ungagged, to hear their full-throated cries in this silent place. It added to the men's confidence. The only security they really needed, he thought, was a *centuria* of well-armed legionaries and the cunt-slave Xara hogtied over the back of a horse. He pulled back his arm and snapped the whip into the tight ass of one of his charges. Fuck him, Viper thought.

They rode on. It was another hour before the Picts walked slowly over the crest of a hill to block the trail. They were tall lean men, painted in a blue woud for battle, and armed to the teeth. Metella said a silent prayer that Xara had reformed, but he also knew that he needed to watch her carefully. He had trapped himself in a hopeless position—he had praised her ability and how essential she was to his plan—and she had somehow taken advantage of that to fuck him with the Atrebates. He could not go back now and disavow her. Somehow, she had outfoxed him, but he would not let her fuck the legion as well.

Metella pulled on her tether until she was standing at the side of his horse, her head forced up in his direction by the tether's pull on her collar.

"Translate exactly what I say, Xara," he growled softly to her. "Or I swear by Zeus that I will hang you by your ankles from one of these trees and flog you to death. Remember, the legion's newest and most vicious torturer accompanies us. He would like nothing better than to assist in your slow execution.

He released the tension on her tether and called out to the Picts, "we come in peace."

"TRANSLATE…!" he ordered her.

Xara repeated his words in the Pict tongue which was very close to that of the Taexali. The two tribes were in fact from the same ancient root and their chiefs were distant cousins.

The Pict leader replied with a one-word question, "Peace?"

He was genuinely confused in Xara's opinion.

"He doesn't understand what you mean by 'peace,' *Ignavus*. Shall I explain it to him?"

She still stubbornly called him *ignavus*, coward, no matter what he did.

He knew that the Picts guarded their territory much more ferociously than the Atrebates. They automatically considered any intrusion by anyone to be an aggression, and act of war.

"Tell him that we bring gifts for the great chief of the Picts, Tininor, and words of peace from the leader of the Roman army that follows us."

Xara translated his words exactly except that she dropped the phrase, "the following army." It was not a good strategy with these people. From what she knew, the Picts enjoyed a good fight; lethal conflict was part of their culture, part of their ethos. Talking about the potential of a bloody encounter with them was more of an inducement than a threat. She had heard stories in Rumabo from the other slaves about how the Picts intentionally started wars simply to give their young men battlefield experience. She knew that they would not respond well to a Roman negotiation that focused on peace. There needed to be more in it for them than peace.

She had tried to explain this to Metella, but his pride had prevented him from listening. He was still upset with the way she had shamed him in front of the Atrebates king, Verica. Ever since the night they had met with the legate, the centurion had kept his distance. In a strange way, she missed his whippings…and his fucking. At least they engaged during those times, during those "learning" opportunities, at least he touched her and....

Yoanie, the gift-slave Metella had given to the Atrebates, had relieved her loneliness for a while, but she had been gone for several weeks. She was now the fuck toy of Togodumnus, Verica's son. The Roman had been cruel to select Yoanie as his gift to Vectus. He knew they were close; he knew they were lovers. There were many other beautiful girls in the horse pen he could have chosen; why had he picked the one girl that she...loved? No, it wasn't love, the girl was too simple to love. But she had grown fond of her and her pointed tongue. The centurion could have left her that one pleasure.

It didn't matter…maybe Yoanie now enjoyed sucking Togodumnus's cock.

"We have an important message for Tininor," Metella shouted out at the Picts.

Xara hesitated. The Pict leader wasn't just acting uninterested, it was clear to her that he saw no point in further communication. No one ever tried to talk the Picts into or out of anything; they enjoyed killing too much. More useless chatter was just going to provoke him to attack. The Roman was blissfully unaware of the danger they all faced. She needed to do something…

"The great chief Tininor will be angry if you deny him the opportunity to hear the Roman offer. He will probably kill you, slowly, for your arrogance in presuming to know his mind," she said boldly,

Metella could detect no hint of fear in her voice.

"Tell him that we want to talk and that we bring gifts," Metella said.

Xara ignored him.

"We have heard that Tininor is quick to give an ignorant man a slow death, one befitting his poor judgment," she shouted.

She had no idea if this was true, but most chiefs had no tolerance for incompetence. She was guessing that the Pict chief would be the same. It was perhaps too daring, but it was the only tactic that madc scnsc to her in the moment. The centurion's approach of trying to persuade them to listen was wrong. She knew it instinctively. Their only hope was to speak directly to Tininor.

"What did you say to them?" Metella hissed, sensing that she had once again changed his words.

"Quiet, *Ignavus*. If you value your life and the future of the Second Legion, let me handle this."

Metella was stunned that she would speak to him this way. Viper moved closer to give her a swipe with his whip, but Metella held up his hand. The centurion had a well-honed instinct for survival. At this point, they needed to trust the girls judgement.

Xara turned back to the Pict, who was glancing to his side. The slave's words would surely find their way to Tininor through his men hidden in the long grass. He hesitated...

"Translate exactly what I say," Metella hissed at her.

"If I do that, we're all dead, *Ignavus*," she said quietly then spat out in a sarcastic tone, "for a slave such as me, death doesn't matter, but for a great man like you, one with your new rank of senior centurion, it would be too much of a loss for the Legion...for the 'civilized' Roman world."

Metella started to respond in a fierce whisper when the Pict leader spoke.

"Tell the Roman to leave his horses and follow," he ordered then slipped behind an outcropping without looking back.

Xara translated quickly with obvious urgency.

"If you want to live, do what he says, *Ignavus*. I know that this man, a field commander, wants to kill you very badly. I can feel it in his words. The only reason he does not do it is that he is now afraid that his chief, Tininor, will be angry. I put that fear in his mind, do not give him a legitimate reason to override that fear and kill us."

Metella heard the urgency in her voice. This was the problem with having an intermediary, he thought, at some point you had no choice but to trust them. He turned and crisply ordered Viper to the ground then he dismounted himself.

"You trust this bitch, Centurion…? I say we leave these three to their fate and use the horses to escape. These savages are too wild; it's like we are trying to negotiate with a pack of wolves. I say…

"Enough," Metella said in a low growl. "Turn and run if you want, Viper, but if I survive, I will mark you as a coward and a deserter."

"You are the one she calls a coward, Centurion," viper answered, as he dismounted.

The fear of the legion's officers executing him for desertion was high on his list of things to avoid. The sentence for desertion in the Second Legion was banishment, to be put out naked in Pict territory would mean certain death, certain slow death.

Xara had already run ahead to the spot where the Pict leader had disappeared into the woods. Metella followed, slowing her with his tether like a hunting dog on a leash. He wasn't about to run after anyone. Xara knew they were in terrible danger. These Picts were ready for war, longing for it. Killing a few Romans and taking their slaves would be nothing to them. She had bought the Roman some time by suggesting that Tininor would want to deal with them personally, but once they had said their piece it would be over. It was likely that the chief was not the voice-of-reason but rather the source of the high-pitched aggression she sensed in his men.

Viper caught up with them at the outcropping. The Pict was fifty yards ahead, waiting. Metella freed Xara's wrist binding then unhooked the tether from her collar.

"If you fuck me again, Xara, I will flay the skin off your body and stake you out for the ants. I swear it by all the gods and by my…"

"Hold your stupid threats for now, Centurion," she said in a tone he had never heard before from her. "These people are looking forward to fighting with you, with your legion. Didn't you see the blue woad die covering their faces. They only wear it when they are ready for battle. Your two slaves are not going turn them from that intention, neither is a wagon full of gold. You should be thinking about what else you can offer them instead of how you will punish me."

***

The chief of the Picts, Tininor, was a young man in his thirties, a war leader. He had more than a hundred kills marked on the spear that rested casually by his side. Xara knew that a young war chief who had personally killed more than a hundred men in battle was not going to be happy with a negotiated settlement with the Romans. He needed victories and the constant urgency of war to maintain his power. A deal, any deal would not be in his personal interest.

She whispered this to Metella.

What she did not tell him was that it was clear to her from the look in Tininor's eyes that he wanted to fuck her. Perhaps his lust would give her some advantage, at least on a personal basis. The Romans were as good as dead though, she thought, telling herself she felt sad that the Picts would deny her the pleasure of killing them herself.

"Greetings great chief," the Centurion started. "We bring the best wishes of the Roman Empire to the Pict people. My name is Senior Centurion Marcus Metella. I command the First Cohort of the Second Roman Legion. I have been sent here by

Legatus Legionis Senatorus Plecio, legate of the Second Legion and Provincial Governor of the Twelfth Province of Briton."

Xara listened to his elaborate introduction then turned toward Tininor and abbreviated it to one line.

"I am Metella of Rome," she said.

She knew the Picts abhorred the pomp and ceremony of government. Strangely, she wanted to give the Roman the best chance to save his life. From the brevity of her translation, Metella knew she had not translated his entire message, but once again he had no option but to trust her judgment.

"He sends you these two slaves taken from a defeated enemy as a gift for your personal use."

Viper stepped forward holding the leashes of the two women. They were still naked of course and he had tied their arms tightly behind at the wrists and the elbows to accentuate their firm breasts and nipples.

"They look like Catuvellauni women," Tininor said angrily to Xara. "Does the Romans know that the Catuvellauni are our cousins?"

He was speaking to her now directly ignoring Metella.

"The Romans view all the tribes as savages. They don't care who is related to whom. They believe that you think with your cock and that beautiful slaves will please you no matter what tribe they are from."

Tininor blinked, he was not used to such talk from a woman. During the rare times when someone in her village spoke of the Picts, she learned that they frequently raided the Taexali villages and took captive. She doubted that the Catuvellauni, distant cousins of the Picts, had fared any better with these wild people.

"What is he saying," Metella asked.

Xara started to relate the gist of their conversation. but the Chief waved his hand dismissively. A Pict warrior took the slaves' leashes from Viper and led the girls away. Xara knew that the war chief would probably give the women to the tribes' best warriors as prizes and that they would treat them horribly. She had heard in Rumabo that the Picts treated their dogs better than their slaves.

At least they will live, she thought. That was more than she could say for the two romans and their collaborator bitch. Metella was still waiting for Tininor to acknowledge the gift. When none was forthcoming, he continued, miffed.

"Our commander wishes to form an alliance with the great Pict nation so that our army can pass through your territory unmolested," he said. "As part of this alliance, we promise gold and the protection of the Roman empire. As our ally, the Picts will continue on as an independent nation."

The Romans were willing to offer the Atrebates and the Picts alliances because these two tribes controlled the relatively narrow stretch of land that connected the north and the south of Briton. Once they had secured this passage with alliances, they would raid the northern tribes and take those who survived as slaves. When they had depleted the supply of northern slaves, Xara know the Romans would then turn on their allies, the Picts and the Atrebates. If the northern tribes united, they would outnumber the Romans a thousand to one, but she knew that was not going to happen.

She translated Metella's words exactly. The centurion was speaking more pointedly now; he had learned from the dialogues with the Atrebates to come directly to the point. But the Picts were not the Atrebates.

The chief spoke a few whispered words to the leader of the group that had stopped them on the trail, and he waved his hand. Instantly, a dozen warriors surrounded Metella and Viper, grabbing hold of their limbs. The Picts had no intention of allowing them to fight to an honorable end.

The chief stood up and spoke in a calm almost disinterested voice.

"Thank you for the gifts, soldier, and for bringing me this message." He paused while Xara translated. "Your words tell me that the Romans are weak, more interested in talking than fighting. We Picts are the masters of these lands. Every tribe in the north fears us. We have no need for your gold and certainly no need to ally ourselves with the Roman empire. Let your emperor come her and kneel before *me* and I will consider making him our ally."

Xara translated his brief speech word for word. There was a Pict warrior at her side with his hand on her collar.

"However, I think it only polite that we reply to your legate's kind offer to spare our lives." He paused and ran his eyes over Xara's body. "You and your subordinate will convey our reply to your leader by having your balls cut off and stuffed into your mouth. Our witches will perform this task after they have played with you for a few days. I shall also fuck your translator while she is useful to us in translating the last words of the Romans we capture in the coming battle. When I have no further need of her, I will bury her alive; it's a fitting end for a traitor, no?"

With a trembling voice, Xara translated the Chief's words exactly for the centurion.

"We came here under a flag of truce," Metella replied evenly, unafraid. "You will dishonor yourself and your people by ignoring the truce flag."

Tininor shrugged after Xara translated.

"Hear me now great chief," Metella continued, "the Roman army camped a few days march to the south is only the first of many legions that Rome will send against you. They will end you and the Pict nation for the outrage you commit today. Remember, it was I, Metella, who warned you of your doom.

For the first time, Tininor seemed to listen to the translation.

"Release us and we will take your refusal to our legate. He will still launch the legion against you, but we will decide the matter honorably on the field of battle. If you torture us, emissaries from Rome under a flag of truce, the emperor's vengeance will only end when the entire Pict nation is dead or enslaved. Ask the Catuvellauni and the other tribes to the south if it is possible to stand against Rome."

Xara translated exactly but there was hardly any need. The centurion's somber tone and his fearlessly demeanor spoke for themselves. Despite herself, Xara had to admire the Roman's courage. He faced torture and a certain terrible death, but he still spoke boldly. Tininor remained silent, but now there was a hint of doubt in his face. Finally, he stepped closer to the centurion.

"Before we cut off your balls, soldier, the witches will drive you mad with pain. They are skilled in thc torture arts. When they finish with you, we will send you back to your legion, naked, riding backwards on your horses, with your balls in your mouths. The sight of you will strike fear into your army. It will tell your Roman legionaries that we are not afraid of them or their retribution. This is much more effective way to say "no" to Rome, isn't that right, Roman?"

Again, Xara translated exactly, the fear in her voice was obvious.

"A man without honor is just an animal, Tininor. I promise you that my brothers will end you and the Picts for this crime. The name Tininor will live on in history as the most stupid of all Picts, the brute who led his people to their destruction."

The two faced each other as Xara translated the Roman's last words. Finally, Tininor waved his hand, and the guards pulled them away. Another guard tied Xara hands behind her back.

"The Romans are cowards," he said to her, "and those that serve them are nothing but slaves."

"Yes, master," Xara answered then at great risk to her own life she added loudly, "Those were also the words of the great chief of the Catuvellauni, Caratacus, who now lies chained in a Roman cage on his way to the Roman emperor for judgement. As you know, most of the rest of the Catuvellauni are buried under the ground."

Tininor turned towards then leaned over until his face was inches from hers. Xara looked at him evenly waiting for his hands to close around her neck.

"Chain her in my hut," he ordered then turned and walked away.

Tininor has no other options, Xara realized suddenly. The Romans would annihilate the Picts one day, either now or in the future. This was the way Rome operated; the romans might use the Picts for a while as allies, but eventually, they would demand their submission.

The centurion never had a chance to stop this war with the Picts, they were too savage, too independent. He must have known this or at least suspected it when they started; he wasn't stupid. It was a moment of startling revelation for her. The Roman, a warrior, had risked his life to prevent a battle that was essentially inevitable, and he had done it for his friends, not for personal gain.

Chapter Four – Pict witches

The guards took the two Romans to a cave at the far end of the village well hidden behind a stand of trees. Metella studies the cavern; it was obvious that it was man made. Ancient members of the tribe must have carved it out over centuries from a massive vein of shiny black rock. He knew that the rock could only be basalt or obsidian—a very hard and very sharp stone that reflected the flickering light of the fire in every direction, creating an effect that was hypnotic and unnerving. It was literally a chamber of horrors.

Just a trick of light, the centurion though, an illusion used to frighten the shit out of anyone unlucky enough to find themselves in this place. He considered his own fear. Yes, he was afraid but also in a way satisfied that he had done his best to avert a battle. He had risked his life so many times in battle—slaughtering scores perhaps hundreds of Rome's enemies, killing so many that he had lost count years ago. This time he had put his life on the line to save others, Roman and savages. This seemed like a good cause to die for; maybe the gods would treat him gently for trying.

There were too many guards to fight, but he tried anyway, grabbing a weapon and killing two of their number before another man could club him into unconsciousness. As Viper watch, terrified, they roughly cut off the centurion's clothes then his and pushed them further into the cave where two wooden "X" crosses were set deep into the stone floor. Viper tried desperately to break free, but a guard smashed him on the side of the head with a spear then strapped him while he was semiconscious to one of the crosses. They did the same to the unconscious Metella.

Rawhide straps held their arms and legs spread apart and firmly against the thick wood. Only their cocks and testicles were free, swinging just below the center of the X. One of the guards prodded Metella's scrotum with the blunt end of his spear and the pain roused him. A small bell rang from one of the side caves and the guards left.

"Where are we…?" Metella asked groggily.

"We are fucked, that's where we are, Centurion, fucked. You and your whore have fucked us for good."

Metella turned his head and stared at Viper. The man had lost it; he was beside himself with fear.

"Take it easy, Sergeant. Their chief was feeling a bit unsure of his decision by the time we finished our parlay. I suspect he will have second thoughts about killing us with the legion on his doorstep. We will be alright."

"ALRIGHT…!" Viper screamed hysterically. "They are going to cut off our balls after they torture us for a few days. Is that what you call alright? You and your whore have killed us."

Metella didn't respond; he was thinking about Xara and Tininor's promise to fuck her while she was useful to him then to bury her alive. Tininor had never intended to negotiate, but perhaps what Metella had said would give him pause.

Something stirred near one of the caves and two beautiful women entered the chamber. Metella had expected old hags, but these two were young. Were they the offspring of those tortured in this chamber, he wondered? Was this a self-perpetuating cult of witches protected by the Picts? Were these beauties fathered by those they tortured?

One of the girls sat by the fire and began to brew a tea of some kind. Soon, the sweet cloying smell of the liquid filled the cavern and steam hung low over the ground. Condensation formed on the shiny walls diffusing the flickering light even more.

The other girl sat by her sister, and they drank prodigious quantities of the brew. It was obvious that they were addicted to it in some way. After a time, they began to sway and to remove their clothes. Soon they were kissing and touching each other sexually as if in foreplay, as if preparing for sexual intercourse.

It's an aphrodisiac, Metella realized. The tea is a powerful aphrodisiac of some kind.

One of the women turned so that they were mouth-to-cunt then they began to pleasure each other with a frightening intensity. Despite the danger, Metella could feel his cock hardening at the sight of their extreme arousal. This was not ordinary lesbian sex; they were ferocious in their lovemaking. He imagined their fierce lips on him, and he shuddered. Was this a prelude to their castration, he wondered, a primitive heathen castration ceremony of some kind? Castrating negotiators was a common way of rejecting a peace offer; Tininor's plan to cut off their cock and balls was not unique. It was not even unusual; he had seen it happen many times in Germania.

Viper kept glancing at him in panic as if begging him to do something. Metella avoided the man's eyes. He had no more moves. The two gift-slaves would survive, he thought, and maybe even Xara as well. Her ability to translate made her as valuable to the Picts as she was to the legion. Even these primitive savages would appreciate this once they began to engage with Rome. As for him and Viper, as the chief said, their last duty would be to carry his answer back to the Roman lines in as horrifying a manner as possible.

It wouldn't do any good of course, Tininor was dead wrong. The Roman legions didn't fight out of courage or fear, their leaders didn't make decisions based on a single atrocity; they would not allow their men to run from the Pict threat. They fought because Rome ordered them to fight and that was not going to change. Rome wanted Briton…all of it.

As for them, if the castration did not kill them, their Roman friends would. Five minutes after their horses entered the stockade, they would be in a medical tent, ostensibly awaiting transport home. But that was just to keep them out of the view of the legion's men. There were no facilities for madmen in Briton and no need for more eunuch's in Rome. More than likely, the legate would order their throats slit and defend it as an act of kindness.

He shuddered at the idea of madness and pulled hard against the unyielding straps. There was no option for an honorable or quick death here. Their suffering was part of Tininor's doomed plan. The man had never intended to negotiate. Their mission had been a failure before it even started.

Suddenly, at the peak of their amorous encounter, the witches separated. One of them took a rawhide cord in her hand and walked towards Metella. She was tall and thin with dark nipples that appeared almost black in the room's steamy fog. He couldn't take his eyes off them. She smiled at him then rubbed the full length of her body, slippery with sweat, against him, all thc time sucking wetly on his earlobe. He could feel her pointed nipples on his chest and her hard clit on his thigh. Her eyes were dilated and black with the effect of the drug. She continued to arch her slim body against his and to stroke his cock to a painful hardness.

Metella pretended she had lulled him into a sexual stupor then suddenly he lowered his head and bit her shoulder with all the strength he could muster. She yelped in pain and tried to jump back but he held on. Her sister approached, saw what was happening, and calmly clubbed him until he released her. Blood was still flowing from her shoulder wound when he regained consciousness. Incredibly, the injured witch looked up at him and smiled, and he understood immediately that their ceremony wasn't just about sex and castration, it was also about pain. The girl dipped her fingers into her blood then put them in her mouth and sucked.

She said something to her sister who moved behind him and roughly shoved a stick between his teeth, tying it tightly behind his neck with another cord. He bit down hard. The wood tasted bitter, it had been too long near the flames and the overflow of their evil brew. There would be no more biting from him.

"For Jupiter's sake, don't antagonize them," Viper cried in panic. "Maybe this is just some kind of pagan ritual. We just need to survive this place for a few hours. The legion will be here soon. When we don't return, they will attack, and we'll be rescued."

He was silent for a few seconds then spoke again with absolute resolve.

"I will personally attend to burying these two witches alive," he said. "That's the only fitting death for creatures such as these. And maybe, before I bury them, I will..."

His voice trailed off as he considered other torments. He was obviously struggling with the situation. His way of coping was to dream of increasingly more devastating methods of torture.

He is also dreaming about rescue, Metella thought. The legion would wait one full day for them to return before beginning their preparation for battle, which would take another full day. Once on the move, the prefect would insist on time-consuming reconnaissance and on a conservative line-of-march. He would never compromise the legion's safety to help anyone, not even me. No, the legionaries would move very slowly and deliberately over the Pict lands to this capital village. It was just too dangerous to allow the Picts to snipe at them or launch a full-scale ambush. He and Viper were on their own, no one was coming to save them for many days.

The girl he had bitten was standing in front of him again with a cup of the foul-smelling brew in her hand. Her sister slipped behind Metella and pulled his head back by the hair. Carefully, almost gently, the first witch poured the warm liquid over his stick-gag to fall unhindered down his throat. They both laughed when he gagged until the liquid started to spill over the side of his mouth then they became serious again. This tea was rare stuff, he reasoned, as they forced him to drink the full measure of the cup.

There was no immediate effect. Other than an awful taste in his mouth, he felt nothing. The witches stood together waiting, exchanging knowing glances. After a time, he felt heat on his skin and began to twist. The two girls smiled and leaned against his body, touching him and each other, kissing with their lips and open mouths. He wondered what had initiated their arousal; when he looked down, he knew. His cock was bursting, fully erect and throbbing, and his balls were swollen to twice their normal size.

Suddenly, he felt an urgent need for sexual release. It was like nothing he had ever experienced in his life. His cock was going to burst if he didn't come. He jerked fiercely on the straps and began to moan with the need. One of the witches ran held the rawhide cord in front of his face so he could see.

The first one barked an order and the other knelt between his legs, his throbbing cock in her face. She wound the cord tightly around the base of his testicles until veins appeared on the surface of his swollen sack then she knotted it. Evilly, she pulled the cord between his balls then wound it again around the base of his cock.

The pain was excruciating, and he started to whine; he had never felt such agony. It was as if she had dipped his cock in boiling hot oil. At the same time, his need for release was so great that his mind was beginning to throb in synchronization with his cock. After a while, his entire body was shaking with the same throbbing rhythm. He had never wanted anything so badly. His mind dreamed of it, yearned for ejaculation.

The first girl, still kneeling in front of him on both knees, gently began to lick the crown of his cock with her tongue. He felt himself shudder at her touch and every muscle in his body tensed for the explosion, but nothing happened. There was no release, no climax, no blissful orgasm, just an enormous pressure in his balls. After a time, he began to scream like a woman.

The second girl knelt between his legs, giggled insanely, then reached up and took his balls into her mouth. Again, he felt the desperate need to come and tensed again with the same result. Her partner in the meantime had slipped his cock fully into her mouth and was pushing her head up and down, exciting herself with the gripping action of her throat. She was fucking him with the urgency of a cat in heat. He could feel everything. This was the greatest blow job he had ever known, but with no release. It was sex gone mad.

Slowly, the Centurion began to cry and plead for mercy. The need to come was so strong that he imagined his semen bursting through his stretched skin. It was an illusion of course. The witches would not allow any physical damage so early in his torture. Neither would they allow him to go mad so soon. Their goal was to take him to the edge of madness a hundred times and with the help of their black tea, they could do it. They had done it before. The entire village marveled at how long the distant wailing of their victims could last.

Metella's torture had just begun. He would be together with the witches for weeks if Tininor let it go on that long. When the time was right, the first girl lifted her leg and inserted his cock into her vagina, a second later the second released the rawhide cords. The centurion felt the first thrust of an enormous ejaculation and his entire body convulsed violently in a mixture of pleasure and pain so intense that after he wondered if he had broken bones. The women, covered in the excess semen leaking from her vagina, stepped back and began to fondle her sister as they spread his cum over their naked bodies. Viper watched this open-mouthed with the terrifying knowledge that he was next.

Metella passed out as they danced and dreamed of his childhood home in the mountains. Hannibal, on his way to conquer Rome, had passed close by the place where he had grown up in Italy. Surprisingly, in the dream the slave Xara was with him, naked and kneeling at his side like a loyal dog. He reached down to run his fingers through her hair then froze as the sound of a wounded animal screamed in the distance. Sound carried a long way in the mountains. Slowly he opened his eyes. It wasn't an animal, it was Viper.

Metella looked down between his own legs. There was a large puddle of blood on the floor, but his limp cock and balls were still there. The effect of the drug were wearing off.

He glanced stupidly at Viper again; he was gurgling and shaking uncontrollable in the middle of the same unbearable torment he had undergone. Metella watched as the witches sucked and coddled his manhood, running their nubile bodies along his. One of them stood up and put her ass near his cock. The other forced the man's swollen member into her sister's asshole. Viper screamed as the girl began to move up and down in a fucking motion as she touched her clit. He tried to resist, tried to prevent further agitation of his abused cock, but the drug was too powerful. The more he pulled away, the more he returned to participate in the agonizing pleasure. He was unable to stop and unable to climax. The expression on the face of the witch he was reaming was pure joy, pure madness. She finally dropped to the floor in a series of incredibly violent shudders. Metella knew that she was climaxing spontaneously.

The other mounted him while removing the cords around his cock and scrotum. He exploded in a wild frenzy of contractions that threatened the stability of his cross. Again, the witches danced around the fire, rubbing themselves with his excess ejaculate.

This could go on for days Metella realized in despair. Between him and Viper and the two witches, they might father a child. Whether they did or not, this indescribably painful process would continue until their cock and balls really did split open from the stress of repeated swelling. When that happened, he was sure that the witches would castrate them and returned them to the legion as mad eunuchs. The effect on seeing him and the fearsome torturer turned into mad half-men would be shocking to the ordinary soldier. Most of the legionaries were more afraid of losing their manhood than their lives. It would affect their ability to fight.

Metella's eyes rolled back into his head, and he slumped forward in despair on his cross. One of the witches made a kissing motion with her mouth signaling him to be patient. They would start again soon. He groaned as she lowered her mouth on her companion's tit. The tribe has bred these two for this purpose, he thought. They were not really witches, probably just the progeny of all the witches who had come before, freakish twins who didn't know anything except this cave and how to use sexual desire to cause extraordinary pain.

They were abominations, creatures that existed outside the limits of human imagination, fiends that surpassed even the most perverse Roman torturer. His only forlorn hope was that their upcoming madness would spare them from more of their evil ministrations.

***

Xara lay naked, draped over Tininor muscular body, her wrists still tied behind her back. Perhaps someday he will free my hands so that I can use them for his pleasure. She wasn't sure what more she could do to please him—he had taken her in th4 mouth the cunt and the ass—but perhaps....

Sexual bondage was not unusual among the norther tribes that never fully trusted a captive even after years of loyal service. She understood that instinct; Brits had long memories and revenge could stay hidden for years, suddenly flowering into stunning violence that was even sweeter because it was so unexpected. The Romans could learn about revenge from us, she thought.

The chief of the Picts was not especially cruel, but he was so physically strong that their lovemaking had been intensely painful. At one point, he had stood up on his feet and just physically lifted her up and down on his rock-hard cock, pumping her. After several minutes, he had come with an enormous bellow and a fountain of white semen. In an incredibly short time, he was up again and performing the same physical act on her asshole.

She had never heard of anyone performing with such animal-like virility and physical strength. This was not the way a normal man, even a Pict chief, had sex, she decided, suspecting that the tea they sipped ritually before bed was an aphrodisiac of some kind.

"You are a bull among men, Master," she whispered truthfully in his ear. "I have never been used as I have been tonight. Your women must worship you."

She rubbed her hard breasts against his wide chest trying to scratch the insatiable itch in her nipples. Tininor grunted. He was awake, too sexually charged to fall asleep immediate, but he was not comfortable speaking with the woman he fucked especially a...

What was she exactly, he wondered? I could make her a slave as the Roman's had done, but I have many beautiful slaves. The one thing I don't have is a way to speak with the invaders. This will be useful once we have defeated the legion and made them our slaves.

His scouts had reported that the Roman legion camped to the south was still preparing to attack. He found that amazing and to some degree worrisome. Unless they were completely stupid, which he doubted, they should be preparing for a siege. No army of any size had ever ventured into Pict land and defeated them. In the total history of the tribe, no enemy had even come close to defeating them. The tribe had ruled these lands for as long as the land had existed. The Romans with their weak men and their colorful uniforms were not going to change that reality.

"Won't you make me a slave, Master?" the girl asked, grinding her slippery vulva into his leg.

"Is that what you want, cunt?" he asked. He referred to all women as "cunt" until he gave them a name. He didn't wait for an answer. "Is this how you plan to avoid the grave? I told the Roman I would bury you alive. Do you want me to go back on my word?"

He stared at her for a moment then continued.

"Where did you learn the Roman tongue?" he asked casually.

He had no place for a traitor in his camp even as a slave. A collaborator was a traitor.

"The Romans took me as a prisoner," she explained. "They put me in with their dogs, and I listened to their conversations. I learned their vile language so I could escape. Unfortunately, I was only able to kill one of them when that opportunity came. The Catuvellauni Tribe game me shelter and allowed me to fight with them against the Roman legion that you now face."

"The Catuvellauni men must have fought like women to be wiped out by these weak Romans," Tininor pointed out rudely.

"They are not weak men, Master. Of course, they are not as strong as Picts, but they have the technology and the tactics to defeat anyone. Rome has conquered every nation and tribe that stood against them. As for the Catuvellauni, they fought like wolves against the Roman legion. Even the Catuvellauni women fought like wolves. I was with them. A Roman took me with a net then clubbed me into unconsciousness after I had killed six of their number with a knife. When I awoke, I was in a slave coffle. They were going to crucify me for killing so many of their number—as my Taexali father had done when they raided our village. The officer you took yesterday tortured me, that's how he discovered I spoke Latin."

"You cut six Romans down in battle with a knife…?" he asked skeptically. "Were they aslccp?"

"They underestimated me, Master. They saw a thin wisp of a girl and a small thin blade and assumed that I was no threat. It doesn't take a lot of strength to run a sharp knife along a man's neck."

Tininor considered her words. They had the ring of truth but also something else. She was hiding something. Few men could deceive him successfully. It was one of the many talents that had led him to becoming Chief.

"The Roman, the one who held your leash, he was the one who tortured you?"

"Yes, Master. He is ambitious. The Romans are quite talented in their use of pain, both as punishment and as an instrument of war. I am ashamed to say that I agreed to serve them as translator to avoid more of his pain."

"You are only a cunt, a woman," Tininor said idly. "We would not expect any more of you."

He was thinking about the Roman's ambition; that was something he understood. He was also considering how he could use this girl; she seemed significantly more intelligent than the others.

"How are you called?"

"My name is Xara if it pleases you, Master."

"You kicked the Roman while you were in his chains...?"

"Yes."

He was silent for several minutes.

"I have need for a translator," he said. "If you serve me loyally and well, I will keep you as my slaves instead of burying you. You will also be available for me to fuck whenever I feel the urge. I enjoyed having you on my cock tonight.

"Despite your warning, I expect to have many Roman prisoners in my hands soon. It will be interesting to hear what they have to say as they beg for mercy. We Picts are also good at using pain."

"Yes, Master," Xara answered.

Unlike the Catuvellauni, the Picts didn't invite outsiders to join their ranks. He had obviously enjoyed fucking her. Perhaps she could use that…

"As you wish, Master. May I ask one small favor?" she said, beginning to lick his growing cock with her tongue.

"Ask," Tininor said cautiously. He had had many slave tongues cut out for asking too many stupid questions and too many favors. It would be a shame to lose this one's valuable tongue to such womanly folly.

“May I join in the torture of the Roman Centurion? He killed several of my Catuvellauni friends by crucifixion. I would very much like to see him suffer as they did.”

He was fully hard now and only half thinking about the implications of her request.

“We have our own torturers, and our own ways.”

“Please, Master,” she said beginning to lick his balls.

Tininor was quiet for a moment, enjoying the feel of her quick tongue on his manhood.

“Why not,” he answered suddenly as she began to push his cock into her mouth. “It's only fitting that you should watch the Roman suffer, that you should watch him descend slowly into madness. No one ever emerges from the black-stone cave with their mind fully intact. You will...ah...ah…”

The chief lost his train of thought as Xara began to suck him off in earnest. She knew that he had reached the limit of his interest in this matter and that further talk would be dangerous. He had given her what she wanted. She moved her body to take him deeper into her throat. She had no choice, he was holding the back of her head and pushing hard. She fought against gagging. Tininor was not a man that forgave weakness especially in the women he fucked.

Chapter Five - Revenge

Xara stepped into the black stone room just as the two women were finishing their third round with Viper. They glanced at her then continued to suck on the Roman's raw cock. Viper was whimpering like a beaten dog, acting very differently from the arrogant torturer who had presided over the suffering of so many. She felt nothing but contempt for him.

The centurion was another matter. His face was set in a look of grim determination as if he intended to defeat the two witches through sheer force of will, but he also looked weak, and his body shook involuntarily every few seconds with orgasmic aftershocks. The destruction of his mind was well underway, Xara thought, staring down at his cock. It was inflamed, swollen to twice its normal size. She could well imagine that every touch from the witches now was a nightmare of withering pain.

She was conflicted. This man had enslaved and humiliated her, caused her to suffer in ways that were beyond description, fucked her like she was an animal. She longed for revenge, but somehow this Pict bondage and torture seemed wrong. Metella was a strong courageous man who the witches were slowly destroying in a manner that was more appropriate for a coward. She wanted him to die, but to die like a warrior—preferably at her hands—screaming and suffering but also fighting. It was...unnatural to see him whimpering like a woman...even unnerving. Somehow it diminished all of them in the cave.

The witches finished with Viper and moved again to Metella. One of them was preparing more tea, the other was laying out the rawhide they used to bind his balls. Xara stood mute for a long time, thinking, then she spoke firmly in their language.

"The great chief Tininor has given me responsibility for this pig's punishment."

The two looked at her stupidly. The drug had captured their minds, she realized. It was probably the same powerful aphrodisiac that Tininor had used in their lovemaking. She sensed an advantage in this and pushed hard, stepping in front of Metella, putting herself between him and the witches. Slowly, she turned and spoke to him in the language of the Picts.

"How do you like the pain of the Picts, Roman? Do you imagine it is like the pain of those you had flogged and crucified? Do you think Roman pain is different from ours…that your suffering is somehow more significant than ours?"

Metella focused on her voice and recognition appeared slowly in his eyes. For a moment his face returned to its normal hardness. He didn't understand her Pict words, but her freedom told him all he needed to know. She had abandoned them and sided with the Picts. He knew he should never have trusted her. There was no surrender in his eyes, no plea for mercy. His body had failed him, but in his mind had remained strong. For him, she would always be the slave and he the master.

"You, you will be on my leash again, cunt," he croaked, "and I promise you that your treason will earn you a punishment that you will never forget."

"Treason," she laughed. She was speaking now in Latin. "How can one allied to pigs commit treason? You are dying a pig's death, Roman. Your cock is already near death. After that, these witches will keep you alive to suffer for as long as they can but eventually you will die. I have no fear of your threats anymore."

He rallied and his voice was suddenly hard and strong.

"Y…you...you were made for the whip, cunt," he spit out fiercely. "You were destined to be a slave. Your body, your mind, your…they all long for bondage, for the ecstasy of a slave's climax. You cannot escape who you are, what you are, and neither can I. What difference does it make if the chains that hold you are mine or another master's? You are a slave!"

Xara grabbed his cock with her hand and squeezed hard. Metella screamed and his eyes rolled back into his head. His reaction sickened and shocked her; this is wrong, she thought, everything about this is turned upside down. Men like Marcus Metella do not scream like a woman. She released his cock but continued to stare into his eyes.

"You know it," he hissed, sensing what was in her mind. "You know that even now you belong in my chains, under my whip."

She stared at him with a look of rage in her eyes as if she were fighting her own inner demons then she turned towards the witch with the cord.

"Bind his prick and bring me his *vitis*, she screamed." (The *vitis* was a short vine-wood staff worn by centurions as a sign of their position and power.)

One of the witches jumped to obey. Long days of intense suffering had conditioned them to respond to authority without thinking.

"We will see who belongs to whom, Roman.

"Bind him," she yelled impatiently at the other witch.

Metella screamed as the witch pulled the cord tight around his scrotum then again as she put it between his balls and over his cock. The skin that remained exposed was bright red with the blood the cord forced to the surface.

The witch tying the cord began to take his balls into her mouth, licking them gently with her rough tongue. The other woman slipped under the cross and began to nibble at the base of his cock. Xara reached down and took the crown of his inflamed cock in her hand. It felt hot and hard.

Metella started moaning. It was an inhuman sound, full of unbearable pain. In a few seconds, he started to scream again, his face a mask of pure agony. Xara stepped back terrified that an act of pleasure could produce such suffering.

"Can you hear me, *Ignavus*?" she asked over his screams. "Do you find this pleasurable? Do you still think that I enjoyed suffering like this at your hand? Do you still think that a woman's suffering is different from yours? Do you beg my forgiveness? I can make them stop if I want."

Metella heard her words and regained enough control to speak.

"I will fuck you again slave and you will feel my whip on your back," he said through the pain.

Xara stayed silent, watching the torture, thinking about his words, about the arrogance of such a man.

"ENOUGH…!" she shouted to the witches. "I want him to suffer for days," she yelled, pushing one of them roughly to the ground. "You are going to kill his mind too quickly with your greedy mouths."

The witch she had pushed scrambled to her knees and resumed her cocksucking. They were in heat from the drug. They desperately needed their own sexual release. Xara knew that in this state they could easily turn on her if she pulled them off him.

"Finish the other one," she screamed, enraged. "He is nothing--a mindless brute. The death of his mind is no loss. This one is more deserving of our careful attention. He must suffer as no one has ever suffered before."

Viper didn't understand the words but the hungry stares of the two witches were clear enough--his time had come. One witch released the cord from Metella, causing a long series of unearthly sounds to come from his mouth then she tied it around Viper's balls. Knowing that this was his final session, she pulled hard. Viper's screams replaced

Metella's in the cave. Xara sat down cross-legged leaning against the Centurion's legs to watch Viper's final agony. Metella's swinging balls occasionally brushed against her face.

Viper lasted a full hour, screaming almost continuously the entire time. In the end, the blood seeping from his cock and balls covered the witches' faces. It was a gruesome horrible end, one fit for a hideous creature such as him, Xara thought.

"A fitting end," she said loudly to Metella when Viper's noises finally indicated that his mind was gone. "Yours will be even more terrible, *Ignavus*. I promise you.

"Sleep now, regain your strength. You will need it in the days to come."

***

Metella slept and dreamed of the battle with the Catuvellauni women and children. "There is no honor in this," he kept repeating to himself in the dream. "No honor for us or for the enemy. War must include honor...without it we are all animals...just...animals...animals tearing at each other with..."

He opened his eyes slowly and lifted his head off his chest. He was still tied by the wrists and ankles to the X-cross and his balls still ached with a pain that knew no end. Viper was moaning a mindless chant, his mind gone. The fire in the cave had burned down, but it was still giving off enough light so that he could see the naked witches sleeping on the floor. Viper's blood covered their mouths and faces; it had spread into a horrid black pool beneath their black hair. He marveled at all the blood. Xara was sitting against the nearby wall holding a curved bronze knife in her hands. The firelight flickered off its wet blade.

That's the ceremonial blade they used to castrate their victims, he guessed, glancing over at Viper. But the man's balls were still hanging from his body. Why was the blade wet if he still had his manhood, he wondered? He looked back at the witches. There was too much blood around them, he suddenly realized, then jerked his eyes back to Xara.

"They destroyed the torturer's mind much too quickly," Xara said defensively, "…and I punished them for their lack of control. Slaves must obey or suffer; isn't that what you taught me, Roman?"

Metella stared numbly at the gruesome scene. Viper was hanging in his X-cross, drooling mindlessly, with the two murdered witches at his feet in a pool of black blood. The image was a vision of Hell. Xara now had him to herself to murder slowly with her knife and her mouth. He shuddered at the thought of what was to come then resigned himself to his fate.

She deserves this reward, he thought. It restores balance in the cosmos for her to extract the same amount of pain from me that I pulled screaming from her lips. She wasn't just an ordinary slave, she was a warrior. I dishonored her by treating her as just another piece of meat. The evidence of her courage is at my feet.

He glanced at her again. There was a vulnerability in her as well as courage, he realized. Murdering these two had not been easy. Perhaps she was thinking of the consquences. Tininor would not take kindly her killing his prized witches.

"Do you fear your death, Roman?" she asked softly. It was a serious question. "Do you fear the unbearable pain I can inflict on you?"

"You will wear my chains again, slave, as I promised," he answered. "You will feel my whip on your back, my cock in your mouth, in your cunt. You were born to heel at my feet, to be on my leash, to wear my gag, and my collar."

Xara stood up with the old rage burning in her beautiful eyes; the dreaded rawhide cord was hanging from one hand, the bloody knife in the other.

"Perhaps I should gag you with your own cock, Roman. Perhaps that would stop your contemptible fantasies. I could do that you know. There's nothing to stop me."

"My prediction is not a fantasy, cunt. You are a fierce, intelligent woman, but you are also a slave. My chains make you feel beautiful and desired; my ropes hugged your body more tightly than any casual lover; my whip reminded you that between us, you are the one who gets fucked, that you are the slave and I the master. There is no equality between a woman like you and a man like me. Your submission is the natural order of things. You know it; that is why you are tormented."

She looked at him strangely then brought the sharp edge of the knife up hard against his balls. One flick of her wrist and she would emasculate him. Their faces were inches apart.

"Don't try any of your tricks on me, Roman. I know that you are trying to provoke me into killing you quickly. It won't work. Your terrible fate is sealed. You will suffer a thousand of Viper's deaths before I'm finished with you."

"Then get on with it, cunt," he yelled angrily in the command voice usually resevered for the heat of battle. "Your cunt threats are beginning to bore me."

There was no fear in his eyes, none. Even now, in his mind he was in command.

She stared at him with growing rage. There was a battle raging in her. Suddenly, she screamed and moved the knife to his wrists, cutting the straps holding him to the cross. His upper body collapsed into her arms. Quickly, she cut his ankles free and placed him on the ground. He was too heavy to carry and too weak to hold himself upright. She lay down beside him on the ground.

"I was wrong. You have courage, Roman," she whispered.

The relief in her voice was obvious. It was as if her inner struggle was now over.

"In recognition of that courage, I will call you 'Master' rather than '*Ignavus*' for as long as we shall live, which I am sure will not be very long."

She turned her face towards his. “Master is what *I* choose to call you, not what you demand I call you, understand?”

He turned his head towards her, his strength returning with each passing second.

“And I will call you ‘Slave,’ cunt. It is the only name that you shall ever have in my eyes,” he answered.

“Which, as I predicted, will not be that long,” she repeated in a resigned voice.

“When they catch us, we will be slowly burned to death. It is the punishment the Picts reserve for traitors, and for those that aid them in their work. It is better that we kill ourselves quickly right here and now. I have a knife.”

Metella rubbed his arms roughly and sat up. He shook his head to clear it then grabbed a nearby length of cloth and wrapped it tightly between his legs and around his waist, fastening it with the bloody rawhide cord that had been used to kill Viper's mind. He was preparing himself to walk, perhaps to fight, something he could not do with tender balls swinging beteween his legs. From the expression on his face, the act of dressing was incredibly painful.

“Get on your feet, Slave,” he ordered in a matter-of-fact manner. “We are not killing ourselves today nor are we going to surrender to these enemies of Rome. We Romans did not conquer the world by surrendering. This is a fact that these Picts are about to find out for themselves. They should be the ones considering suicide, not us.”

He took the bronze knife from her hand.

"Dress yourself and find something for our feet. We won't get far in the hills without some protection, and build the fire up again, we need to make it seem as if the torture is proceeding normally in here."

Xara obeyed without comment. When they were ready to leave they both stood in the middle of the cave for a moment. Suddenly, Metella reached for her and crushed her to him, delivering a long delicious kiss on her mouth.

"When we return, I will make your mouth pay for it's insolence towards my cock," he whispered into her ear.

"My mouth has no fear of your torture, Master, and neither do I. I am confident that we won't live long enough for you to make good on your promise. The Picts are the best hunters and trackers in the world. We have no chance in the hills, none. Perhaps you should exact your revenge now..."

He looked at her once more and smiled then released her from his arms. She lowered her eyes and silently stepped to his side half a step behind, the slave position.

Chapter Six - The Return

The journey back to the Roman lines was a nightmare. As Xara had predicted, once Tininor discovered the carnage in the cave, he became enraged and decided to personally lead the search party to recapture the two fugitives. Almost as an afterthought, he ordered Viper's mindless body bound and cast into a campfire. As terrible as this death was, it was a mercy for the suffering torturer.

But tracking a man as skillful in combat as Marcus Metella was not as easy as the war chief had anticipated. The centurion and his she-wolf slave always seemed to be half a step ahead of him and his men. When the Picts finally did manage to close on the pair, they ambushed a string of his men with silent efficiency and ruthlessness. The roman and his bitch were fighting for their lives and like any cornered animal, they fought fiercely. It wasn't until the fourth day that the Picts managed to trap them.

"I want them alive," he told the Pict fighters assembled around their campfire. "There is no way out of this gully and the sides are too steep to climb. "Capture but do not kill them," he added with an ominous warning tone. "I want to hear their screams as the flesh is slowly burned off their bones. I want..."

The sudden appearance of a lookout interrupted his rant. The man was unable to speak. He didn't need to speak; the nearby sound of a Roman bugle said all that was necessary. The Romans had trapped Tininor and his men in the same gully.

At first light, Tininor looked up at the sound of birds taking wing and saw the air full of Roman arrows. He was one of the first to die when an arrow pierced his throat. Cornered and leaderless, the Romans made short work of the Picts. Metella emerged from the nearby woods just as legionaries were killing the last Pict. His slave, Xara, following behind.

"Hail, Centurion," the leader of the *centuria* saluted.

"We were on patrol...looking for you and scouting ahead of the main column," he explained. "The Picts were so busy herding you into this gully that they didn't see us take up positions behind them and on the ridge. They were easy targets for our archers in this clearing.

"This is a glorious victory," he added. "We should take heads."

"Gather your men, Centurion," Metella ordered, "IMMEDIATELY!"

As the legion's senior centurion, Metella was technically entitled to take command of the patrol.

"There will be no heads taken. We are returning to camp this moment. I want your men to prepare to move fast, to discard everything they are carrying except their weapons. We need to get to the column as soon as possible."

The officer blinked once then saluted and turned to obey sensing the urgency of the centurion's words, but Metella wasn't finished.

"...And bind and collar my slave...painfully by her wrists and elbows. When we return to camp, I want you to cage her in the smallest cage you can find. I will attend to her punishment when we have finished with the Picts. She has much to answer for."

The young centurion saluted again and literally ran off to attend to the Centurion's orders. The journey back to the Roman lines was quick but uneventful. Metella immediately presented himself to the prefect and the legate, who were meeting in the command tent planning the battle.

"I have vital intelligence, gentlemen," he declared simply then began to spcak.

It was nearly an hour before they finished and emerged from the tent.

The centurion's report, which precisely located the Pict village and its defenses was incorporated into the battle plan. His confirmation that their chief, Tininor, had been tracking them and had been killed in the skirmish with the scouts was a key piece of military intelligence. The prefect had planned to surround the village and to soften up the Pict defenses over the next few days.

"This plan is now obsolete thanks to the centurion's intelligence," Lepidi told the legate. "We must attack now from all sides using the full force of the legion in an all-out assault. They will be leaderless for a few days and therefore unable to mount any kind of organized defense."

He was right. The attack on the village was a slaughter. The warriors fought bravely, but without any organized defense, the Romans isolated their small groups of men and quickly overwhelmed them.

After the battle, the legion moved through the village mercilessly killing all the men. The women and children were quickly gathered into slave coffles and sent south. When it was over, the legate ordered the bodies of the Pict warriors hung in the nearby trees as a warning to other Picts in the area. As Metella had predicted, the legion's commander was incensed and outraged that the Pict chief had refused to honor his truce flag and killed his emissary.

"The story of our victory and our retribution will travel," he told Metella. "It's a good object lesson. The next group of Picts will not be so quick to fuck with us when they hear about the fate of this village.

"We have taken more than a thousand slaves—a number uunprecedented in the Roman conquest of Briton. Their sale will allow us to give every man in the legion a piece. You are going to be a hero for a while Metella.

"How can I reward you for your contribution to this victory, Centurion?" he asked, grabbing the centurion's elbow, and turning him away from the hanging Pict bodies. "I think a heavy purse filled with gold would be appropriate, eh?"

Metella turned towards him and snapped to attention.

"I was only doing my duty, Legate, so I will only accept the prize awarded to centurions."

Prefect Lepidi, who was standing nearby, laughed knowingly and the legate smiled. For all his intelligence and courage, Metella was naïve sometimes.

"...However," Metella continued, "I would like to personally own the slave Xara, the translator. She will perform better for us, I believe, if she knows that she has one master. Being owned by the legion is rather...impersonal and has resulted in me having some…disciplinary problems with her."

The legate nodded his understanding. Public slaves were always more trouble than private ones.

"I was thinking the same thing the night you brought her to my tent, Metella. She needs a firm hand and an occasional whipping from one master. She also needs to be fucked occasionally," he added bluntly. "You can't deny these savages their relief for too long. They will turn wild on you. They are like animals you know."

Metella's face turned red at the mention of fucking the girl. He already fucking her. He was also unsure that he would ever be able to fuck anyone ever again given the tender condition of his balls.

"You have served the Second Legion well, Metella," the legate continued. "I give her to you as a reward for your service against the Picts under the condition that you continue to use her in service to the legion."

Metella nodded. "I am a soldier, Commander. Neither of us is going anywhere."

***

Xara hung painfully by her wrists tied to the tent's main pole. Her long toes were barely touching the dirt floor. Metella had kept her in a small cage covered with a bearskin during the entire Pict campaign. Three days of near-total sensory deprivation and excruciating muscle pain had softened her, he hoped. This was her first real contact with anyone since their return to the legion.

From the way she was stretching her naked body in her current wrist suspension, it was clear that she welcomed even this limited form of freedom.

The Centurion entered the tent and stretched out on his cot, ignoring the girl hanging beside him. She stared down at him with the same old hatred. He had bested at least a dozen Pict warriors during their time in the forest. His skill with the sword and his courage were undeniable, even for her. He was the reason they had survived long enough to be rescued. He had saved them from Tininor's flames.

She knew now that they would never be lovers or even friends. They were much more than that—he was her master and she his slave.

"You are now officially my private property, Slave," he said unemotionally staring up at the tent's top. "I can legally whip you or fuck you or kill you any time. Remember that."

He was quiet for a while then he sat up on the cot and remained still for several minutes collecting his thoughts. When he spoke, there was a finality to his words and a strange sadness.

"For freeing me from the Picts and for your help in the hills against Tininor, I promise you a quick death should I ever decide to end your life. You will never face the cross, the stake, the flames, or any other excessively painful death at my hands, even if one is warranted. Do you understand?" he asked, turning towards her.

"Yes, Master. I understand perfectly. My reward for saving your life is a quick death whenever you decide I deserve it. That is very generous of you."

He searched her face for the sarcasm that her words implied, but her expression remained neutral.

"However," he continued, "for the disrespect and the suffering you forced on me and for ordering the witches to kill *Principales* Spurius Vipsanius, Viper, I condemn you to a life of slavery and suffering at my hands, with no possibility of emancipation."

The girl looked at him and incredibly she smiled, flexing the hard muscles in her bare ass.

"You are too generous, Master, allowing me to serve you and to suffer as your slave. Rome has been too kind to me my entire life. I feel unworthy to accept such a gift."

Metella knew exactly what she was saying. She would never acknowledge her slavery, not to Rome, not to the legion, and certainly not to him. She was a free person, a warrior whose current reality was to be the chained prisoner of a Roman officer. She called him master of her own accord, as an acknowledgement of his warrior skill and strength. She would never surrender to him willingly, never.

They were both quiet for several minutes. Finally, she spoke again, softly.

"I am grateful to you, Master, for allowing me to serve you given the terrible damage done to your manhood."

Metella' hand moved protectively to his midsection. He had been afraid to use his cock for anything but pissing since their time in the cave. It felt fine, as if it had restored itself, but he had avoided any erection in fear of the reaction. If an erection did occur, he ignored it. The psychological effects of the cave torture still lingered. His fear was that the torture had left him impotent.

"Are you a eunich now, Master?" Xara asked bluntly. "Is your cock dead? Has your terrible experience with the Picts turned you into a woman?"

There was a hint of a taunt in her voice and Metella began to feel angry. Even though she had saved him, she had also participated for a while in the torture that had left him this way. Literally, her hand, even if it was done as a subtrofuge against the witches, had contributed to his condition.

Enraged and frustrated, he leaped to his feet and grabbed a nearby cane, laying a dozen quick strokes on her bare ass and legs.

"You fucking bitch," he hissed. "You are partly responsible for the way I am."

"You...you hit harder now, Master," she panted, "...now that you are a woman. I have heard that this is the case. Eunichs punish their charges harder. It is probably because they are frustrated by the loss of their manhood, by the loss of life's greatest pleasure. It seems only fair that they..."

He couldn't believe his ears, the bitch was still taunting him. He ripped off his pants and without thinking turned her around and shoved his rockhard prick into her cunt, lifting her six inches off the ground. The girl wrapped her legs around his waist and began to pull herself up and down by her bound wrists, gently tightening her grip on his member with each upward stroke. In a few moments, he exploded. She shuddered in climax at the same instant, biting softly into his shoulder with the passion of a desperate lover.

For once she remained silent.

After a while he freed her from the pole and took her to his bed.

Chapter Seven - Vindolanda

The Roman fort at Vindolanda took two-and-a-half years and only one-thousand-five-hundred lives to build. The commander of the Second Legion, *Legatus Legionis* Senatorus Plecio, considered this a bargain since the lives lost in its construction were Pict slaves, whom he had already condemned to death for their ongoing rebellion against the empire. With the practical need for workers, he had deferred the death sentence for anyone who agreed to work on the fort.

Originally, he had wanted the fort's walls and guard towers made of timber from the Great Northern Forest nearby to shorten the fort's construction time to six months, but Prefect Lepidi's strong objections and the savage Pict attacks on the wooden fort with fire arrows ultimately convinced the legate that they needed a stone fortification. To accomplish this, Legate Plecio moved the legion's camp fifty miles east, adjacent to a quarry where, according to his architects and engineers, the right stone was available.

Of course, the most essential element for the construction of a stone fortress at Vindolanda was labor. After the defeat of Tininor and the total destruction of his capital village, the estimated eighty thousand Picts in the northern regions were leaderless and disorganized. Plecio took full advantage of this temporary condition by attacking other Pict village and taking the men who survived as slaves.

It was only when Lepidi pointed out that the Pict resistance was stiffening and becoming more organized that he stopped. By that time, however, they had all the slaves they needed to build the fortification that would enable them to hold onto the northern land they had won. The two thousand men and fifteen hundred women the Romans spared for this purpose was the number Lepidi estimated they could control in building the fort.

He was right again, in addition to three major attacks from the renegade Picts still roaming the region, they had had to put down a rebellion of the slaves. With typical Roman brutality, they crucified one hundred of the leaders to convince those remaining that leading a rebellion against Rome came with a high price.

Legate Plecio formally pardoned the slave Xara of the Taexali for her complicity in the death of *Principales* Spurius Vipsanius, Viper, after the senior centurion of the First Cohort, Marcus Metella, described the help she had given him in escaping from Tininor and his witches. As he had promised, as a reward for his escape and the invaluable intelligence he provided the legion, Plecio also officially transferred ownership of the slave Xara from the legion to the senior centurion.

Metella whipped the girl every night for a week after her trial and left her hanging naked by her wrists outside his hut so that legionaries passing by could see the marks of her suffering. Strangely, as many noted, she didn't seem as unhappy as the marks would indicate she should have been. The rumor was that the centurion's revived cock provided her with generous compensation for the pain.

Senior Centurion Metella never spoke of it. In fact, he didn't participate in any of the soldier's gossip that flew through the camp after their victory.

***

"You will take a cohort of cavalry south, Metella, meet my wife and daughter at Rumabo Imperium, and escort them through the great forest here, to Vindolanda. They will be living with me to make the point that we have truly pacified this northern region."

Metella stared at the commander in shocked disbelief. The had *not* pacified the region around Vindolanda; if anything, the Picts had gotten bolder in the last two years. The only reason the five-thousand men of the Second Legion survived against the eighty thousand Picts still roaming the hills were the high stone walls and the four enormous gate towers—each a castle itself—that controlled access to the fort. The farms surrounding the fort and the heavily armed hunting parties they sent into the forest to forage allowed them to survive, but they were far from pacifying the area.

"This example, will encourage the men to take wives and begin to transform the fort into a true Roman settlement."

Metella was quiet. It was obvious that the commander did not want his or anyone's opinion.

"You will leave in two days. Dismissed."

"Yes sir."

Metella walked directly from the legate's office to Prefect Lepidi's spartan quarters.

"Has he gone insane...?" Metella asked. "Does he really think that we have pacified this region? Is he actually going to bring his wife and daughter into this hell? We are losing men every week to the Picts. Docsn't he read the reports?"

"Sit down, Marcus. You need to learn the reality of Second Century Roman politics."

Metella sat, still shaking his head. He hated politics and politicians. They represented everything bad about the empire.

"The *legatus legionis* is under great pressure from Rome to make progress in pacifying this region and to begin to make contributions to the empire's coffers. The Second has not sent a substantial number of slaves south since we sent Caratacus and the Catuvellauni prisoners, and they were more symbolic than substantial. By pushing too hard and too fast with the fort's construction, Plecio has decimated the ranks of the Pict slaves we could have sent. Now that the construction is complete, we must once again begin a campaign to bring the Picts to heel, which will produce new slaves and generate income for the empire. The one thing you need to remember, my boy, is that it is all about the money.

"In the meantime, however, Plecio must convey the impression to Rome that we are in control, and that sending them more slaves is simply an administrative matter of harvesting the population, which is cowed and submissive. There's no better way to do that than by bringing his family here."

Metella was still shaking his head.

"Politicians manipulate reality to get what they need; soldiers cannot do that. We need to deal with reality no matter what the perceptions."

"He is going to get all of us killed by perpetuating a lie," Metella countered.

Gaius Lepidi shrugged; he had been battling enemies and politicians for almost as long as Metella had been alive.

"Fortunately for the *legatus legionis*, Rome's watchdog, *Tribunus Laticlavius* Artimus Concerti and his protégé, Tribune Atticus Versus, have hitched their stars to Plecio's star, and their independent reports to Rome have supported his distorted version of the truth."

"None of this makes any sense to me, sir. Eventually, when we lose, the truth will come out that five thousand Roman legionaries cannot defeat eighty thousand Picts and who knows how many other tribes that we have yet to invade."

Lepidi shrugged again.

"He is hoping that we can turn the situation around in the meantime."

"How?"

"By forming alliances with the other tribes and using them as mercenaries against the recalcitrant, especially the Picts."

"If we turn the other tribes into allies, won't that reduce the number of slaves we can capture and send to Rome?"

Lepidi didn't bother even to shrug; the answer was obvious. Rome's days in Briton's north were numbered if the northern Britons continued to oppose Rome with the same ferocity. The conquest of the north was simply too expensive for the benefits Rome derived.

"Go and get the legate's family, Centurion, as ordered. We, unfortunately, are pawns in the perception game now being played with Rome."

***

Xara no longer followed the centurion on a tether tied to his saddle's pommel. Nowadays, she rode her own horse and followed half a length behind his. She had also clothed herself, not in anything elaborate, but in furs and belts that allowed her to move freely without exposing her private parts. The men of the First Cohort and the attached cavalry unit, though of her as a mascot—still a slave, but one who performed the important military function of intelligence gathering. Something that they could not accomplish without a translator.

The centurion, however, didn't care what they thought. Xara was his personal slave, his concubine, and his communicator. She kept them alive as she had kept him alive in Tininor's basalt cave. What a legionary though of him or her was unimportant if he followed orders.

"We will make camp here, Sergeant," Metella said to his new sergeant, *Principales* Galerius Tullas.

The man shouted out an order and others of lesser rank echoed it. The column stopped and men began to organize for an overnight stay.

"I need to visit Togodumnus, Sergeant. I will be back before nightfall."

"Sir…"

Tullas understood without asking that Xara would accompany the centurion to translate.

They turned their horses off the path into the forest and the column soon lost sight of them. Metella waited until the Atrebates following the column appeared at their front and he followed. The Atrebates, perhaps wisely, had never disclosed the location of their village to the Romans. Metella often wondered how they managed to find it with any references that he could see. The only reference they knew about in the Great Northern Forest was the north-south trail they followed, which Togodumnus permitted them to use as part of his tribute deal.

"Greetings, Roman."

Metella turned to the side and found Togodumnus standing in front of a tree leaning on a spear.

"Greetings, Chief Togodumnus," Metella answered formally.

He had delivered the two annual tribute payments to the Atrebates since they formed their alliance, but Togodumnus had not appeared either time. Metella had attributed his absence to the presumed turmoil that must have followed the death of his father, Verica, who, according to Xara, had died of natural causes.

"I see you still have your fuck slave," he said, and Xara translated.

"Yes, do you still have yours…the one you offer visitors?"

They both knew he was referring to the whore that, with Xara's help, Togodumnus had used to ridicule him.

"No, I sold her, but I still have your gift, the one you know as Yoanie. She is still a fine sheathe for my sword…every night. She is the best I have ever had…so tight she can pull the essence out of my cock without using her hand, and such a soft mouth. I whip her sometimes just to feel her tremble in my arms. My wives, however, are jealous of her sexual skills and they make her life miserable."

Metella nodded. They had had enough small talk.

"My men and I are riding south through the forest, and we will be returning by the same route in a fortnight, perhaps less. I am informing you of this, so our passage does not cause you any concern."

It was standard procedure to let the Atrebates know when a Roman column was passing through the forest. Togodumnus, however, didn't answer or otherwise acknowledge the message. Instead, he stared at Xara.

"I see your slave rides a horse these days. Is she still a slave? Does she still service your cock?"

Metella was surprised by the question. The chief of a tribe did not usually concern himself with a slave.

"I still remember her," Togodumnus said quietly. Such an arousing look..."

Xara continued to translate despite the content of his words. In the last two years, she had begun to trust the centurion's judgement. He knew, almost as well as she did, the meaning of the northern people's words and their temperament.

"Metella didn't answer, nor did Xara."

"Would you consider selling her to me," he asked. "I have a man who is now familiar with Latin. I will trade him for her plus a suitable quantity of Roman gold of course."

Metella hesitated. Xara wanted to turn towards him, but she knew that would make him look small in Togodumnus's eyes. She had already done enough damage to their relationship by misleading Metella about the tradition of kissing the whore's ass.

"No, thank you," Metella said quietly. "I am comfortable that her translations are now...accurate. This took me a long time and many whippings to achieve."

Togodumnus said nothing and his expression didn't change. He just turned and disappeared into the woods. His men led them back to the Roman camp.

"There is something not right in his head, Master," Xara said as they dismounted.

"I know," Metella answered. "I don't trust him either, but he is not going to jeopardize his tribute by doing something stupid. He knows what happened to the Picts."

"I would not be so sure of this, Master. The Atrebates have owned the Great Northern Forest since the beginning of time. They don't place the same value on gold that you Romans do. You have upset the balance with your victories over the Taexali, the Catuvellauni, and the Picts…anything is possible now."

Metella didn't answer. Xara had a sharp mind and an uncanny ability to see behind the words, but there was nothing they could do even if she was right. Rome was committed to its current strategy, and they were simply executing orders.

Chapter Eight - Lollia Plecio

Xara became increasingly more agitated as they approached Rumabo. She had told Metella that she had been a Roman prisoner before the Catuvellauni had rescued her, but she had never said where they had held her as prisoner. He had assumed it was a rough camp with loose security, but as her skittishness increased, he guessed it had been Rumabo. Which seemed strange—the slave depot at Rumabo was incredibly secure, slaves, especially beautiful slaves destined as sex slaves, didn't just walk away from such a place.

But he had more important things to think about—Commander Plecio's misrepresentation of the Pict danger at Vindolanda for one, and Togodumnus's strange behavior in the forest for another. Then, of course, there was the problem of making two high-born patrician women of Rome comfortable on the arduous journey back to the fort. Xara's strange behavior was the least of his worries.

"Do you want me to whip you?" he had finally asked her. "You are behaving as if you're concerned about something. What is it?"

"I do want you to whip me, Dominus. I want to forget everything except the pain and the pleasure of you. DO IT…!"

He had grabbed her hair, stripped off her furs, and put her across his knee. The spanking that followed had been memorable, both in its intensity and in her reaction. She had slipped off his legs crying and trembling then had gotten to her knees and sucked his cock and balls.

She had done that many times, of course, but this was different. It was as if she saw an end to their relationship and wanted to get everything she could from these last few times. For example, she never stared at him while she was sucking his cock; it was just something that she was uncomfortable doing, something too far over the line of surrender. This time she mouthed his balls then looked directly into his eyes as she masticated them. The effect on him was instantaneous and extreme—he wanted to fuck her, to insert his cock into one of her holes, it didn't matter which, and ram it until he ejaculated in a massive orgasm that would set them both back on their heels.

But she wouldn't let go. She insisted on sucking his balls until he was on the verge of exploding then she took his cock in her mouth and sucked with furious intent. He came with a bull-like bellow as she continued to suck. He finally had to pull her off.

"What has gotten into you? Are you bewitched?" he had asked her after as she lay naked in his arms.

"I just want to please you, Master…to please you."

He knew she was not telling him the full truth, that there was something on her mind, but he also knew that there was no way to get it out of her. He would just need to wait.

***

Lollia was annoyed. Her whipping bench was only half the size of her mother's. How was she to maintain discipline with such an inadequate device, she wondered, fuming? In Rome, she had had access to the family's punishment bench in the garden; it had the proper length and gave her cane full access to her handmaiden's ass, thighs, calves, and feet.

But this, this…inadequate stool was barely long enough to hold the girl's torso…and the straps, they were set far too low, forcing her to kneel to secure the girl's wrists and ankles properly. It was an impossible imposition, grossly unfair. This entire journey was unfair, her father ordering them to this wilderness was unfair.

"TAKE OFF YOUR CLOTHES AND LIE DOWN, CUNT! I don't have time for any more of your foolishness."

Her mother would chastise her for using such crude language, but she had the right. Arria was just a cunt, a cunt with the body and legs of a woman attached…and she was totally inadequate for someone of her rank. Her mother descended from the Bruta line—one of Rome's oldest and most honorable families. They were patricians, or as her mother was fond of quipping, patricians to the patricians.

She would have had this girl on the block and replaced in a day if they were still in Rome. She was a rough and rural Greek, comely enough, perhaps beautiful to some, but completely lacking in any of the skills needed to serve a high-born lady of Rome.

"Lie down."

Arria obeyed and Lollia quickly knelt and tied her wrists and ankles. Fortunately, the bench did have rawhide cords to tie her tits to the sides which she did, pulling hard in frustration. The tit cords would hold them against the rough wood if she wanted to cane the sides, which of course, she did.

She had no choice but to train the girl herself—all they had for sale in this godforsaken town were savage Britons. It would take her months to train a Briton in even the most basic tasks. Her father's decisions had forced her to work with what she had. Arria, a Greek, was impossible, but she was better than nothing.

"When I tell you to draw a bath, Arria, you…will…make…sure…that…the…water…is… warm."

She punctuated after every word by delivering a devastating cane stroke to the helpless girl.

"Now perhaps you will remember."

"When I tell you to wash my feet, you…will…have…a…basin…ready…for…this…p urpose.

Each stroke of the cane caused her bound body to jerk wildly on the bench.

"Remember…"

When I order fruit, you…will…test…its…firmness…and…confirm…it …is…ripe.

She moved to the other side of the bench and targeted the side of her bound tit.

A good slave, a slave to a patrician such as I, learns…anticipates…and…moves…quickly…to…s erve. Understand…?

"Yes, Mistr…"

She had not finished her response before Lollia began to cane the soles of her feet. For a moment, the pain prevented her from catching her breath and screaming.

"You will improve, or I…will…make…your…life, even…in…this…wilderness, a living hell."

The girl was twisting, writing as the agonizing pain flowed into every part of her body.

Back in Rome, the senior ladies had explained to her that a slave was, *"servus non habet personam"*—a non-person, an animal without personality, without property, who doesn't even own her own body, who has no family, no ancestors, no name, no nickname, no rights. A slave could not even give legal testimony without being tortured to ensure his or her testimony is truth.

"You stay there for a while and suffer, Arria. Think about your duty to me, your obligations to me. Later, I will ask you questions and, depending on your answers, continue your punishment."

Lollia walked to the window and stared out over Rumabo Imperium. It was dirty, too dirty to even venture outside. There were soldiers and slaves everywhere. The northern part of the town served as a depot for slaves, a place where the legions brought raw public slaves, Brits, and where auctioneers sold them to private buyers from every corner of the empire.

Rumabo was a major commercial center for the Briton slave trade…not at all suitable for a Roman patrician.

She held her scented handkerchief to her nose. The smell from the slave quarters was devastating. After a while, she turned back to Arria. The girl was crying softly, still moving in a vain attempt to moderate her pain. Lollia picked up the cane and moved into position; she still had large areas of skin with no marks. She wanted the girl to suffer sufficiently so that she would not need to go through this again…it was too much work.

***

"Senior Centurion Marcus Metella at your service, Mistress. Your husband, *Legatus Legionis* Senatorus Plecio, legate of the Second Legion, has ordered me to escort you and your daughter north to Vindolanda. I am at your service."

Gegania Bruta Plecio looked down at him over her nose with a haughty stare. Soldiers from the ranks, even high-ranking officers like a senior centurion, were just one small step above common plebs from the streets. They were not people whom someone like her or Lollia would normally associate.

"This is my second in command, *Principales* Galerius Tullas, and my translator, Xara of the

Taexali. She will assist you during the journey in matters where a man's presence would not be appropriate."

Gegania didn't bother to even glance at the sergeant, she just stared at Xara.

"…a prisoner?"

"Xara is not a prisoner. She is my personal slave whom I lease to the army for translation services," Metella replied evenly.

"A slave whom you allow to carry a Roman knife."

Metella had given Xara back her long sharp dagger as a condition of her service. They had found it in Tininor's camp. It was the least he could do.

"We will be leaving in the morning, mistress. I have secured a covered wagon and horses for you. Please be ready."

"One wagon will not be sufficient, Centurion. There are five of us—me, my daughter, and our three handmaids. They and our clothing and personal effects will fill a second wagon. We also have some essential furniture that will fill a third wagon."

"As you wish," he said in a strained voice, "…With your permission."

Metella bowed and walked away. Sergeant Tullas and Xara followed.

"Requisition two more wagons and horses, Sergeant," he ordered when they were outside.

Xara waited until the sergeant had left then spoke.

"Taking three wagons through the forest will be dangerous, probably impossible," she said quietly. "Even one small wagon is going to be difficult. You should have said no to her."

Metella turned angrily towards her.

"A centurion does not say no to the wife of a *legatus legionis*. She will need to order me herself to leave the extra wagons behind, which she will do when she sees the width of the trail."

When Metella was angry like this, it was better to be far away. Xara nodded and moved away into the street's shadows. The thought that someone in Rumabo might recognize her was preying on her mind. It had been two and one-half years since she had escaped from this place, but the Ninth Legion was still stationed here, and Romans had long memories, especially for a slave who had killed a legate. Fortunately, anyone who knew her in those days knew her as the dog-girl, the one who lived with Sextus's mastiffs. She now looked and acted completely differently.

She hoped...

***

Sextus Reburras, the Ninth Legion's *primus pilus* stared across the desk at Senior Centurion Metella. They had the same rank, but it didn't matter—Sextus was responsible for the legion's wagons, and he was refusing to allocate three heavy wagons for Metella's mission. The Ninth's new commander had promoted Sextus only a year ago from his position as the legion's *dux carnifex*, its chief torturer, to his new role of quartermaster, and he was not going to allow Metella to waste precious wagons. They were essential for transporting slaves south.

"I am sorry, Metella, I wish I could oblige you, but I do not have three wagons to spare. You will need to make do with the one I gave you. You know, it will be difficult to get through the forest trail with one wagon, taking three through the forest will be impossible."

Metella stared at him annoyed. Of course, he knew that what he said was true. They didn't have the men, horses, nor the equipment to drag three heavy wagons over tree stumps and out of ditches and soft ground. Getting one through would be difficult enough.

"I need your help, Sextus. The commander's wife insists on having three wagons for her entourage and her belongings. I know that once she sees how impossible and dangerous this is, she would relent and allow us to leave the extra wagons behind."

"Leave the wagons behind…!" Sextus said angrily. "Are you crazy? Do you know how many slaves we send south every week? I need those wagons!"

Metella was silent for a moment, thinking.

"Listen, send some of your men with us. As soon as the commander's wife sees the problem and relents, they can drive the wagons back to you. It will only take a few days… It will be worth the time to keep our two legates happy, no?"

Sextus hesitated.

"Neither of us wants this lady to go to your commander and make this into an issue, right? This way, we keep her from backing him into a corner. Believe me, if we leave Rumabo without these wagons, this will become a problem. She is just looking for an excuse to vent. Apparently, she is here under protest."

"Who wouldn't be 'under protest' after being summoned from Rome to Vindolanda?"

They both smiled. The legions' centurions almost universally acknowledged that patricians in the military were trouble.

The next day, Sextus delivered the two wagons and the four men he had seconded to Metella's cohort. Xara stepped quietly and unnoticed into the background. Sextus, her former master, and the man who had sentenced her to live with the dogs, was the one Roman in Rumabo Imperium who was sure to recognize her. Even in the shadows, he might remember her face. Neither Metella nor any of the Second Legion's officers would be able to save her from the cross if that happened.

Roman law demanded crucifixion in the most painful and longest-lasting manner possible for a slave who killed her master. She had no idea what they would do to a slave who killed her master after castrating him with her teeth—they would probably bury her alive in a box with an air tube to ensure that madness comes before death. In either case, their punishment was something to avoid.

Ironically, it was Metella, her protector, who called Sextus's attention to her. He was obviously confused why she was hanging back and kept looking in her direction, which caused Sextus to stare at her as well. Suddenly, she knew for sure that Sextus had recognized her. She put her hand on her dagger, prepared to end her life easily rather than submit to their torture.

It was at this moment that Gegania and Lollia Plecio arrived in their hired chairs followed by their three handmaidens, Calpurnia, Cluntia, and a limping Arria, still weak from her recent caning.

"We should leave, *immediately*, Centurion," Gegania said. "The smell of soldiers and slaves is deeply offensive to me and my daughter."

Metella dismounted and led the way to the first wagon where the driver had arranged pillows and cushions for his passengers. Sergeant Tullas led the handmaids to the second wagon where they would share an uncomfortable space with the ladies' clothes and personal effects. Legionaries had already loaded the third wagon with their furniture, including the matching mother and daughter punishment benches.

Sextus continued to stare at Xara, who remained in the shadows. Metella mounted his horse then finally noticed their strange exchange.

"Is something wrong, *primus pilus*?" Metella asked.

"Your…translator, where did she come from?"

"We captured her after the battle with the Catuvellauni at Wolf's Glen."

"Before that…?"

"She was a prisoner in a Roman camp. She escaped and was taken in by the Catuvellauni."

"What camp…?"

"Why all these questions, Sextus…? She saved my life when I was a prisoner of Tininor of the Picts…that's all I need to know. His body was tense, ready to spring at the centurion if necessary. Was this what Xara had been hiding; was this why Xara had been acting so strangely during their trek south."

"Why all the questions, Centurion…?" he asked again in a more insistent voice.

Sextus stared at him. During his time as the legion's chief torturer, he had overseen the horrible deaths of hundreds of prisoners, but he had never enjoyed it. He thought of it as a job, just another difficult duty that a Roman soldier sometimes draws. Not only that, but he also never liked *Legatus Legionis* Lucius Flaccus, the prior commander of the Ninth Legion at Rumabo. Flaccus was a sadist and a rapist. He had secretly applauded the commander's gruesome and cringe-worthy murder; it was entirely fitting. Had the exhaustive search the legion conducted caught the perpetrator, he would have crucified her with all the pain and suffering his considerable skills could have produced, but now, almost three years later…

"I am surprised that you didn't emancipate her after such a heroic act, Metella," he said quietly.

"There were other factors involved," the centurion answered vaguely.

Sextus turned towards him and nodded.

"Have a good trip back to Vindolanda, my friend. I will expect to get my wagons back in a few days."

Sextus saluted, glanced once at Xara, and spurred his horse. Metella looked at Xara, now emerging from the shadow, but he didn't say anything. He had heard about the murder of the commander of the Ninth Legion, everyone had, but he had never imagined that Xara had been involved… Suddenly, he remembered how many times she had sucked his cock; how many times he had come in her mouth with a joyous bellow. It was better to let sleeping dogs lay.

Xara was staring at him, her face white. He nodded casually then rode to the front of the column and she followed.

Chapter Nine – The Great Northern Forest

"I want her strangled," Lollia said evenly. "If we were in a civilized place with reasonable facilities, I would have her tortured and sold, but here in these never-ending woods, I must be practical. Just have one of your men take her into the forest and strangle her. She is impossible to train; I will have my father or my fiancé, Tribune Atticus Versus, buy me another."

Gegania stood slightly behind her daughter silently applauding her adult behavior. Dealing with an incorrigible or incompetent slaves was one of the many duties a high-born Roman woman must learn. Lollia was only eighteen, the same age she guessed as her slave, Arria, but she was already a firm hand in dealing with her.

The loss of their two wagons had been a severe blow and a disappointment to Gegania. It was also, Xara suspected, the reason for Arria's "intolerable behavior." Riding on a horse with a man, even a disciplined one like Sergeant Tullas, was too much for the libido of some oversexed slaves. His closeness had obviously overwhelmed and intoxicated the girl, provoking her to exhibit and unacceptable deportment around her young mistress, Lollia.

"Is there a problem with my daughter's order, Centurion? We are the legal owners of the girl. If we want her strangled, what's the problem?"

Metella glanced at Tullas then at Xara. He had already had one run-in with Gegania over sending the wagons back to Rumabo. Even after she had seen the difficulty in dragging three wagons through the forest, she refused to allow him to return them with their belongings to Rumabo. It was only when Metella pointed out that the Atrebates savages were not tolerant of delays, nor did they respect the patrician's rank…as he did. He assured her that they would enslave her and her daughter if they attacked.

The legate, who had an intimate personal knowledge of the difficulties of the forest path, might forgive him for sending the wagons back, but he would not forgive him for losing his wife and daughter in a raid…or for disobeying her direct and legal order to strangle the handmaid. A slave's owner had the right to order her death for cause…and it did not matter what the cause was.

Sergeant Tullas was a good soldier, but it was entirely possible that the girl's hands had found their way into his pants during their long ride, or that his cock had found its way into her vagina atop his mount. It was also possible that her new infatuation with Tullas's cock had caused her to be terse or even insubordinate with her mistress, but was this good reason for killing her?

It was Xara who finally broke the stalemate by taking the girl's arm.

"Take her into the forest, Xara, and do it. I don't want the men to see," he ordered, knowing that Xara would never obey such an order.

She pushed Arria away from the wagon. In seconds, the pair disappeared into the darkness and all that they could hear were her final pleas for mercy. After a time, even these stopped.

"Good," Gegania said, assuming Xara had done as they ordered.

She turned with Lollia and returned to their wagon.

***

Xara pushed the slave into the woods until they were out of sight then she forced her roughly to the ground and built a small fire. The soldiers had bound Arria's hands behind her back then tied her elbows together to make her even more helpless.

"Where are you from," Xara asked, playing with her dangerous looking dagger.

Arria didn't answer; she couldn't speak. She had heard the centurion's decision and the order he had given his woman. The knowledge that she was facing her killer, that Xara was going to strangle her was terrifying. Xara took a length of rawhide cord from her pouch and wound it around her hands.

"You heard…my master ordered me to strangle you, but I can give you a few more minutes if I find those minutes interesting. Otherwise, I will just do it now…like killing an unwanted kitten."

Arria continued to stare, her eyes wide with fear, but she didn't say anything. Xara rolled the trembling girl onto her stomach and wrapped the cord around her neck.

“Gr…Greece…the island of Limnos in the Mesogeios Sea,” she blurted out, “The sea the Romans call Medius Terra, Middle Earth…the Mediterranean.”

Xara tightened the cord until only a small amount of air was passing into her lungs. She knew that Metella had passed the decision about the girl’s life to her, that he was torn between obeying Gegania and his sense of Roman fairness. however perverted it was. Turning the decision over to her was the only way out. She relaxed her grip. It would be less painful for her to slip her knife between the girl’s ribs into her heart. Death would be almost instantaneous.

“Greece…? Where is Greece?”

“I…I don’t know how to answer your question, Mistress. Greece is near Rome, a few days sail,” Arria said in a trembling voice, suddenly understanding that her answers were keeping her alive.

“Tell me how you came to be here…in this forest.”

“My mistress brought me here. You were there, in, ah, Rumabo Imperium.”

Xara was curious, but she knew that a quick death was not going to be enough to satisfy her curiosity. She stripped off the girl’s tunic then positioned her on her back. Using rawhide cords, she tied her ankles and knees to two stout tree branches to keep her legs open. While Arria watched, she found another branch with just the right strength and flexibility.

"You have information in your head that interests me, sweet Arria, but you are not sufficiently motivated to tell it to me in the time we have available so…"

She sat on the ground and crossed her legs then lifted Arria's head into her lap. The girl's soft inner thighs were immobile and well within the reach of her pine switch.

"Please, Mistress, I am not…"

"*Shhh*...Just answer the best way you can. I will provide the motivation."

"Now, how did you come to be here…?"

"My…my mistress brought me with her from Rumabo."

The switch lash out at her soft inner thighs.

"Think, Arria. Why would I ask a question if I already knew the answer? How did you come to be here?

"My…ah…my mistress ordered me to come from Rome…?"

The switch struck her again in the same spot.

"Where is Rome…?"

"I…I don't know…I don't know. Rome is five day's sail from Greece…then…then a day's wagon ride from the sea they call Middle Earth."

"How large is this sea…?"

"I don't know."

Xara hit her again then a second time on the other leg.

"It's, ah, at least big enough to take five days to sail…"

She hit her again.

"Please…"

…and again.

"I, ah, I heard someone say it too ten days to sail from Rome to Egypt and…five to sail to Spain."

"How long did it take you to sail here?"

"I don't know! I DON'T KNOW…!"

She gave her another vicious blow to stop the growing hysteria.

"A full cycle of the moon," the girl screamed, her lovely legs twitching.

Xara stopped to think. Thirty days…Rome was a thirty-day sail to the south then it was another five days to Greece, five to Spain, and ten to Egypt—wherever those places were. She had imagined that Rome was just on the other side of the Western Waters. She had once thought about traveling to Rome to kill Romans, but now she realized that the Romans here in her land were far from their own.

"Why are you with the Romans…?"

"They took me…I was working in my family's vineyard when Roman soldiers came. They killed my father, raped my mother, and took me and my brother as slaves. I spent five days on a ship and five in a cage in Rome then a guard stripped off my clothes and made me stand on a stage. The man who bought me locked a collar around my neck and put me in a coffle with two other slaves. He delivered us to the House of Plecio where he ordered me to serve the Lady Lollia."

Xara remember her own introduction to Rome, in the Taexali village of Devana, where they had killed her father and crucified her mother.

"How much do you want to live, Arria."

"I, ah, I want to live only I…"

She struck her thighs again, hard.

"This is a hard place, Arria, only those with skills, a purpose, and a fierce determination to live can survive here. They kept me in a pen with their dogs and I used that time to learn their language and to learn that my purpose in life is to kill Romans."

She swiped her again, angry.

"How much do you want to live, Arria."

"I will do anything to live."

"Then prove it…"

Xara turned the girl over onto her stomach until her face was buried in Xara's cunt. The soft round globes of her ass were well within reach of the switch.

Slowly, she began to whip the girl's luscious globes.

Xara didn't say anything, she just kept switching her ass until she felt Arria's tongue licking her labia. She let it continue for a while then…she whipped her again. The girl immediately buried her tongue deep in Xara's vagina then her ass then she began to suck furiously on her clit.

Xara switched her another few times then lay back and let Arria serve her.

The pain, the arousal, the bondage all combined to drive Xara then Arria into orgasm…then twice more. It was not until the moon was high in the sky, hidden somewhere above the trees, that Xara untied her and hid her in the supply cart under a pile of extra blankets.

"I will bring you food and water. We will be in Vindolanda in three days. I will find a way to hide you there, perhaps Sergeant Tullas can help. He seems quite fond of you."

"Yes, Mistress," Arria purred.

The switching and the girl-on-girl sex had made her numb with…she didn't know why she was numb, only that she was.

"Stay hidden. Your life depends on it," Xara said then she was gone.

***

"Did you do as I ordered?" Metella asked when Xara crawled naked under his blanket.

"Would a well-trained slave disobey her master, Master?

"Is that what you are—a well-trained slave?"

"Of course, let me show you."

She reached down and found his erect cock then straddled him and slipped it into her cunt.

"I am you slave, Master, your well-used property…" she whispered in his ear while her vaginal muscles squeezed, urging him to full hardness and length, "…especially when you are inside me, especially when we are joined like this."

"I thought you hated all Romans," he said huskily as she started to move.

"I have everything that is Roman. I hate the very idea of Rome, but I have developed a taste for some Romans."

She bent over until her nipples were scraping against his chest then reached out and put her mouth over his, all while maintaining the rhythm of their lovemaking. She enjoyed the hardness, the sharp edges of his body as he did hers. At just the right moment, she instinctively squeezed her vaginal muscles and he shuddered with the first of many contractions. She felt his shudder and allowed herself to climax. He continued to thrust for a long time, and she continued to service those thrusts with a sublime feeling of tightness.

After, she rolled over onto her side with her head in the crook of his arm.

"Where did you put her?"

"In the supply cart under some blankets. When we get to the fort, we will need to find someplace for her to hide."

"I have already spoken to Sergeant Tallas. He will put her with the Pict women in the kitchen until we have another column heading south then he will find a way to smuggle her out with them. He seems quite fond of her."

"How did you know I would not kill her…as you ordered?"

He shrugged in the dark.

"I didn't," he said simply. "I just assumed that you knew me well enough to know what I really wanted."

"I know you, Master. I know every inch of you. I have the taste of you in my mouth all the time. Nothing good lasts very long in this place, but I am happy now…with you."

There was nothing left to say.

The Picts attacked their column next day.

***

There was no warning, no angry beating of drums, or whooping war cries, no drugged-up, blue-woud faces, no priests dancing a wild jig just the sudden whoosh of arrows cutting through the air and men falling in pain. Metella knew there were savages following them—they always followed them through the forest—what he did not know was that these were Picts not men of the Atrebates. Seventy of his men fell in the first barrage, forty in the second as shields rose automatically to form the *testudo* (tortoise) defense.

But the Picts were waiting for this. They immediately launched a frontal attack against the *testudo* formations that killed another hundred Romans. By the time the Romans switched to a line-abreast, the attackers had once again melted back into the forest. Metella used the time to consolidate the line and bring the column into a tighter defensive position.

Xara followed the Picts into the woods as Metella knew she would. She was too light to carry a Roman shield, nor was she comfortable in a defensive role. In the forest, she could become invisible among the trees, striking out at the enemy with her pointed, razon-sharp blade. Her speed and quickness made it seem as if a ghost had come into their midst. In all, she managed to stab or slice two-dozen warriors. She didn't know how many of these wounds were fatal as she didn't stop to assess the damage, but they were all incapacitating, which was all that counted in the middle of a battle.

Despite her efforts and the Romans, the Pict strategy of arrows followed by frontal attack was working. No matter how many the Romans killed, there were others to take their place. Metella had stationed himself near the Plecios' wagon, knowing that his first duty was to protect the legate's family.

"TAKE US OUT OF HERE WITH THE CAVALRY!"

It was Gegania, the commander's wife, screaming at him from the relative safety of the wagon's underside.

"PUT MY DAUGHTER AND ME ON HORSES AND TAKE US OUT OF HERE!"

Metella sent two messengers running down the column and took a knee near Gegania.

"Your responsibility is our safety, Centurion. I demand you get us away from here."

Metella stared at her for a moment. It took him that long to turn his mind from the battle to what she was saying.

"You need to stay hidden, Mistress. These savages only plan for the first few minutes of an engagement. We will have this fight under control soon. Just stay calm."

"I will not stay calm; I want you to…"

Metella spied a group of Picts attacking the supply cart and carrying it away as his men tried desperately to form up. Romans didn't fight without orders, formations, and tactics. He moved away to take personal command of this part of the defensive line and organize a counterattack to retrieve the wagon.

Out of the corner of his eye, he saw Lollia break away from her mother and run for the horses.

"GET BACK…!" Metella shouted, but it was too late.

The girl ordered one of the men guarding the horses to help her up and she raced off down the trail. It was exactly the wrong thing to do. Half a mile away, a group of Picts stationed on the trail speared the horse, throwing Lollia to the ground. The man in charge was smart enough to know that she was too valuable to kill and ordered her bound and brought to the rear.

As suddenly as it started, the raid was over; the Picts melted into the forest and disappeared. More than half of the soldiers in the ambushed column were dead or severely wounded. A search party led by Sergeant Tullas discovered the supply cart a short distance away. It was empty; the Picts had also taken Arria.

Xara stood next to Metella and Gegania stood a short distance away when Sergeant Tullas made his report to the centurion.

"One hundred and seventy-five dead, eight wounded seriously, one missing, and the contents of the supply cart—all of them—taken. Should I organize a cavalry troop and go after them, Centurion?"

Metella looked at Gegania then back at Tullas.

"Where would you go, Sergeant? In what direction would you search? Men on horses in these woods would not have a chance. Even if you found them, they would pick you off one by one. Get the men organized and have a horse harnessed to the cart. Lady Plecio and her handmaids will ride in the cart. We will leave the wagon and its contents behind."

Gegania walked away, her face stone. Tullas saluted and hurried to do as Metella had ordered. Xara stepped closer to Metella and spoke to the side of his head.

"These were Picts in Atrebates territory…," she said quietly.

"A raiding party. They must have seen us enter the forest and decided they could ambush us on the way out. It was a good plan."

"Yes, but how did they get Togodumnus permission to enter the forest."

"They didn't," he said quietly, turning towards her. "They just slipped in without his knowledge."

"Nothing happens in the Great Northern Forest with the knowledge of the Atrebates and their king. You know this. I would guess that the treaty between the romans and the Atrebates is over."

He stared at her.

"All I know right now is that I have lost two girls to the Picts, two girls whom I was responsible to protect."

Xara shrugged, preferring not to argue the fine points of his statement.

"In a day, Master, the Picts will know that one of their prisoners is the daughter of your leader. You should be thinking about what they will do with this information."

Chapter Ten - Pict Revenge

No one blew any horns or waved banners. The Picts were simply there when the hazy sun rose over the bogs…by the thousands. Too many for the Roman cavalry to disperse or for the infantry to fight in an open-field conflict.

"What do we do…?"

Legatus Legionis Senatorus Plecio, the commander of the Second Legion, had never pretended to have much military skills. If anything, he gave the impression that he viewed the Roman legions and the legionaries as unpleasant necessities. Many high-born patricians, even those serving in the Roman army and the navy, shared this aversion although publicly they praised these warriors as heroes.

"We should turn the catapults on them," Tribune Atticus Versus hissed.

The legate had not addressed the questions to him, but he felt he had the right to an opinion in this matter as Lollia, the girl the Picts had taken in the forest, was his betrothed. They had never met, but the legate had felt that a marriage between the Plecio and the Versus families would benefit both. This marriage opportunity was one of the main reasons he had ordered his wife and daughter to Vindolanda.

"What do we do…?" the legate asked again, turning directly towards the *praefectus castrorum*. Prefect Gaius Lepidi was effectively in charge of military matters for the Second Legion. It was a role that not only required a superb grasp of battlefield tactics but also a sophisticated understanding of the legion's military and political interests. This success of this union was one of the principal reasons Rome had conquered the world, or most of it.

"Nothing…" Lepidi answered quietly.

"What do you mean 'nothing,' Prefect," Concerti shouted. "We cannot ignore this; they are issuing a clear challenge to us by assembling this many savages and bringing them to our gates. If we do nothing, we will encourage more organized rebellion."

Tribunus Laticlavius Artimus Concerti was the legate's political advisor and the next-in-line commander of the legion.

"Behind these walls, Tribune, we have the advantage. They only outnumber us three or four to one—not enough to take the fort. If we were to go outside these walls and challenge them in the open, however, we would lose the advantage. They might beat us. In addition, we would need to use the entire legion to execute such a maneuver, which means that if we were to lose the fight, we would lose the fort as there would not be enough of us left to defend it. Let me repeat that, Sir, we would lose Rome's farthest permanent outpost in the north."

"We must fight," Versus said, stepping between the prefect and Concerti.

"HOLD…! All of you," the legate said sternly. "This is my decision, my daughter."

He had little patience for anyone, political or military, who argued their positions too vehemently. He considered extreme views a challenge to his authority.

"We will wait and see what the savages have in mind. Have everyone report to their attack-posts, Prefect, full loads to all archers, and ready the catapults to repel a mass assault."

Lepidi nodded and gave the orders to his adjutant.

"It would be good to have the senior centurion leading the First Cohort if we have to fight, Legate. The men respect Metella; they will fight harder for him, and we will..."

"NO...!" the legate said, highlighting the finality of his decision by turning away.

The legate had ordered Metella imprisoned pending trial for "cowardice and ignoring his responsibility" during the attack in the forest. Gegania had reported that he was responsible Lollia capture; that she had urged him in the height of the battle to take them away on horseback using the cavalry, but that he had frozen, refusing to leave the safety of his men. Her word, that of a patrician, counted for a lot.

Lepidi remained silent. He knew that the legate's wife's accusation had trapped the legate, normally a fair man. The commander owed his appointment to his wife's powerful and influential family—the Brutas—without them, he could not continue as the Second Legion's commander.

Time...

The prefect knew he needed to let some time pass, to let the pain from loss of his daughter ease before pressing Metella's case. The man was a senior centurion, with many honors and medals, the hero of their recent battle with the Picts, and the primary reason for the defeat of their enemy. He had every hope that he could get the charge dismissed if he kept a cool head.

He was wrong.

***

The Picts waited until the sun was high and most of the haze had burned off before putting the stakes in place. They were crude poles, recently cut, but they sent a spike of fear into the heart of every Roman watching. The Picts left the stakes standing for almost an hour.

It was a brilliant strategy, one designed to increase the horror of what was about to happen to its highest level. Xara, now temporarily the slave of Prefect Lepidi, watched with growing despair. She knew that what was potentially about to happen in the bog would threaten Metella's life and hers. There was already talk that Tribune Versus, the equestrian, or perhaps Concerti, the political advisor, should control her, the legion's translator. She would never serve either of them. Much more than Metella, they represented the true evil of Rome.

No Romans would never pardon Metella if…

The penetrating sound of Pict horns drew everyone's attention back to the stakes. Suddenly, the Pict line opened, and warriors dyed with blue woad carried two naked girls—the blond haired Lollia and Arria, her handmaid.

They held them over their heads so that their nakedness was visible to every Roman on the wall. When they got to the stakes, two men held their backs against the wood while another tied their wrists over their hears behind the stake. On command, then men lifted the girls and fit their wrist ropes inside slots cut high on the backs of the stakes. The two hung there, suspended two feet off the ground until two other men tied ropes to their ankles and fit the ankle ropes into slots cut behind their waists. They splayed them open, their skin taut awaiting the flames.

Lollia was screaming, but the sound was too far away to hear. It was obvious though that she was begging the soldiers on the wall to help her. Arria just stared, perhaps more familiar with abuse.

"We must do something to save her, NOW!" Versus shouted, "before…"

The commander turned back to Lepidi, whose face was chalk white. He knew what a burning would do to his plan to free Metella from the legion's dungeon.

"Well…?"

"This doesn't change the, ah, military assessment, Legate. I am sorry, but the risk to the legion and to this Roman asset is too great to try to rescue them. I am sorry."

“Sorry…SORRY! You old relic,” Versus shouted. “Who cares if you are sorry. The savages have a lady of Rome, a highborn lady of an ancient and noble family. We must help her; we must!” He turned towards the legate. “Let me take a cohort of cavalry out, sir. We can race there and be back in less than two minutes. It’s worth a try…she is your daughter!”

“You are dismissed, Tribune Versus, and ordered to remain in your quarters.”

The legate turned and nodded to two nearby guards, huge men who immediately moved to Versus side. When he reached for his sword, they grabbed his arms and forcefully walked him down the stairs to his quarters, where they stood guard.

During this incident on the wall, the Picts had piled bundles of dry grass and kindling at the bases of the stakes. Lollia had started screaming in a high-pitched wail that everyone could hear. Once again, the Picts waited, drawing out the horror of the moment. Arria continued to gaze off into the distance. One of the Picts stepped forward and caned her across her protruding mound and under her tits until she too was screaming.

There was no attempt to communicate, no movement until a Pict stepped from the line with a torch. Without hurrying, he lit the dry grass beneath Arria and stepped back. Lollia stopped screaming and watched as the flames rose higher. There was no wind. When the fire touched her skin, she let loose an unholy shriek that seemed to go on for hours.

No one moved. The Picts waited until the fire had consumed all the wood, flesh, and bones then the man with the torch returned and stood in front of Lollia's stake. The legate stood paralyzed, watching. No one said anything. Suddenly, the Pict with the torch turned and flung it in the direction of the Romans.

Immediately, four of the blue woad men reappeared and threw aside the grass, lowering Lollia to the ground but not untying her bonds. A long pole appeared, and they pushed it between the girls bound legs and her arms then the four of them lifted it in the arm. She hung on the pole, her long blond hair scraping the ground, her long body bent by the pole. The line opened again, and the pole carriers walked through. As one, the enormous assemblage of Picts turned and followed the polemen until the surrounding hills made them invisible.

There was no ambiguity about what they had seen. The Romans knew the Pict's had spared the girl from the flames to make her suffer for as long as they could. It was a symbolic gesture to burn her handmaid; to suspend her from the stake, to carry her away hanging from a pole. Their new war chief, Drust, had made sure that every Pict present and those within the range of his messengers knew that he had captured the daughter of the Roman chief, and that he would hurt the roman legate through his daughter until he could reck his vengeance directly on him.

That same day, Xara slipped over the wall and disappeared into the late afternoon fog that settled over the bog. The next day, a military tribunal heard the charges and evidence against Senior Centurion Marcus Metella and convicted him of cowardice and failing to follow orders in protecting the family of the legate.

In a weak attempt to make the proceeding look fair, the commander recused himself and forbid Tribune Versus, the girl's fiancé, from serving on the tribunal. Instead, he appointed *Tribunus Laticlavius* Artimus Concerti as chair, *Praefectus Castrorum* Gaius Lepidi, and *Decanus* (Corporal) Mamercus Placididius Pictor as members of the panel. He chose the corporal at random from the senior ranks of legionaries "to represent the men in the ranks in this sad business."

The vote was two to one for conviction, although most of the men of the Second Legion felt that Concerti had applied undue influenced on Corporal Pictor to get him to vote guilty. Concerti sentenced Metella to loss of rank, scourging, and banishment—a death sentence in this region. After he read the formal sentence, Concerti added that he hoped the savages would burn the former *primus pilus* as they had done to Lollia's loyal slave, Arria.

The legion's *dux carnifex*, its chief torturer, carried out the sentence the next day and Metella staggered out the gate just before sunset. He was naked and his back was cut open from his shoulders to his calves. With his last bit of strength, he managed to stagger a hundred yards from

Vindolanda's walls. He didn't want any of the legionaries to see what the savages would do to him. They had already seen enough.

***

Xara hid in the high grass outside the fort. She knew the Romans; she knew what they would do to Metella for the crime his he supposedly committed. They were a spiteful people, for all their greatness, they retained a streak of spitefulness that made them small. The centurion had obeyed orders his orders to keep the legate's family safe; if Lollia had followed his order and stayed under the wagon, the Picts would not have taken her. As for cowardice, everyone in the legion knew that the centurion was the bravest of them all. If anything, his courage had saved them that day in the forest.

Yet, here he was, punished.

She watched him crawl away from the gates and wondered where he got the strength. The torturer's whip had laid open his back. He didn't want the men to see him in this condition. She would need to wait until night; she was a fugitive now. Once again, she had escaped from Roman clutches, but this time, she would be the hunter and they the prey.

She knew what she needed to do. There was only one option for them now. Gegania's false testimony and the legate's grief over his daughters capture and torture had forced them to ally with the Picts. She wasn't sure they would have them; they had a new leader now—Durst, but it was their only choice. They could not survive hunted by both the Romans and the Picts.

Chapter Eleven – Treason

Metella was only semi-consciousness for several days. At first, all he could do was mumble a few incoherent remarks, but over time, he improved, eventually managing to open his eyes, drink tea, eat, and eventually walk. Everyday Xara worked a special grease, concocted by one of the tribe's medicine men, into his skin to maintain its pliability and to stave off infection—the likely cause of death after being scourged. Xara's care and the grease saved him.

"Wherc am I?" he finally asked on day five.

"With friends," she answered.

"We have no friends in the north. Where am I?"

"You are in a Pict village, Master. They will allow us to remain until you are well enough to travel then perhaps, we can walk to the sea and take a ship to Egypt."

"Egypt…?"

He stared at her as if she had gone mad. How did she even know about Egypt and why would they go there? He wanted to ask more, but he was too weak. Xara insisted he drink another cup of tea, another concoction of the Pict priests, and in minutes, he was asleep. She knew that sleep would restore his strength, she also knew that this was the last day she could hide the truth from him.

"Where did you learn about Egypt," he asked her the next day.

“Arria—the slave girl they burned—she told me. She was from Greece, but she said she heard soldiers talking about Egypt and Spain, which are almost as far from Rome as Briton. We can go there together, Metella, and leave all this madness behind…”

He tried to sit up but only managed to get to his elbows. She helped him, propping him up against the wall of the hut.

“Where am I, Xara, and why are you here?”

“As I told you yesterday, you are in a Pict village. They are allowing us to remain until you are well enough to travel. I left Vindolanda the day before your trial. I had no desire to become the slave of a Roman tribune. Both Versus and Concerti are assholes. You know this.”

He stared at her for a long time trying to understand what she was saying, trying to fit it together with what he remembered. His mind was still not functioning well. Slowly, he organized his thoughts into a priority order.

“Why are the Picts helping us?”

“You are the enemy of Rome now, Master. You wear the proof of this on your back. The new chief, Drust, believes that the enemy of his enemy is his friend or at least his ally.”

“They have forgiven us for killing their witches…for killing Tininor?”

She shrugged.

“They didn’t say anything about that and neither did I. It happened years ago.”

“Two years…”

She shrugged again and looked away. He knew there was more.

“What else…?”

“I made a trade with them.”

“What trade…?”

“Information. I told them about the fort…it’s weaknesses, and they gave us sanctuary.”

He stared at her for a long time. He didn’t have the strength to be angry.

“Why would you do that? It is treason.”

“Treason for you perhaps, Metella, but perfectly reasonable for me. I never swore loyalty to Rome, only to you. Rome has always been my enemy. It will always be my enemy…”

He continued to stare.

“I did it to save your life, Master.”

He raised his hand to her throat but did not have the strength to squeeze.

“So, your plan is to betray Rome, heal me, and run away…?

“My plan is still unfolding, but that’s a fair summary of where it stands right now.”

“You would abandon your home, your fight…?”

There was a long pause. Xara was not comfortable talking about her feelings.

“For you I would, yes,” she said. “The larger question is, ‘would you do the same for me?’—would you abandon your people, your legion…for me?”

He didn’t answer and she didn’t press him. She didn’t want to hear his answer. She gave him more of the sleeping tea and helped him back onto his pallet. That night, she licked his cock as he slept and was relieved to see it respond with an erection. Knowing his aversion to waste, she sucked on it, gently massaging his balls, until he squirted cum into her mouth and his body shuddered in a healthy male orgasm. She swallowed then lay back on the pallet, her arm slung over his bare chest. Somehow, she knew that an ending of some kind was coming for them.

The next morning, Metella stood on his feet for the first and staggered to the door. Outside, he saw the normal workings of a Pict village and something else. The Picts had stretched Lollia out over a drying rack. She was naked and had cane marks crisscrossed over her back. The marks were faint—they clearly wanted her to live with the pain for weeks or months if they could manage it—but the look of suffering on her beautiful face was obvious.

"Your information must have been valuable for them to spare us her fate," he said quietly.

Xara, who was standing behind him, didn't respond. She felt no guilt for what she had done. The Romans had always been her enemy. She had put her hatred of them aside for a while, during the time she was with Metella, but his false trial and his banishment had rekindled her enmity. Rome was not just the enemy of anyone who refused to kneel, but it also ate its own. Metella was the most loyal and effective Roman she had ever known, and they had turned on him. There was no way she was ever going back.

"Has your plan unfolded anymore, Slave?"

"No," she answered quietly. "My plan depends on you and…on what's in your heart."

He turned and walked back to his pallet.

"I want to talk to their leader, this Drust," he said. "Can you arrange that?"

"Yes," she answered quietly then turned and left the hut.

She knew what his answer would be to her question…she had always known. The legion might reject Metella, but he would never reject the legion. They would never see Egypt together.

***

Drust sat cross legged in front of the fire. Beside him on her knees was Lollia. His men had bound her arms tightly behind her back at the wrists and elbows and crossed and tied her ankles. They had also fit a noose around her neck, tied it over one of the huts horizontal poles, and terminated it around a stake near Drust's leg. The rope prevented her from sitting back on her haunches, which over time created a burning pain in the small of her back. Whenever he wanted, he could pull on the rope and cut off her air.

Drust was eating a piece of meat from a small animal, a rabbit perhaps. Every few minutes, he would tear off a small piece of meat and feed it to the naked girl. Xara sat in the back behind Metella.

"It appears that you are going to live, soldier," Drust said, initiating the conversation.

"…Thanks to my slave and your medicine, and of course, thanks to the sanctuary you have provided. I owe you my life."

"No, you don't, Roman. Your life was our part of a trade I made with the Taexali girl."

He glanced at Xara.

"Picts always honor their word. Everyone in the north knows this. Normally, I would have cooked you over one of our fires and eaten your heart. I saw how you fought in the forest. I would have welcomed your strength and your skill."

Metella nodded, acknowledging the gruesome complement.

"May I ask how Picts came to be in the forest of the Atrebates, chief?"

Drust stared at him for a moment then pulled on the rope forcing Lollia to stretch her lovely body to breathe.

"Why not…? We are allies now, are we not?

"I gave the Atrebates chief, Togodumnus, son of Verica, a choice, fight us or the Romans. He choose to fight the Romans. The Picts have a long history of working with the Atrebates tribe. He has voided the treaty his father struck with Rome and joined us."

Metella stayed silent sensing that the chief had more to say.

"We will win this 'war' with Rome, Centurion. For all its many faults, Rome is rationale. Every day we resist Rome's conquest of the north, we reduce its profits. The benefit of conquest—slaves—remains largely fixed while the cost keeps increasing. At some point, it will simply be unprofitable for Rome to continue. I persuaded Togodumnus of this and he forsook the Roman gold and allowed us to execute the ambush."

Metella remembered Prefect Gaius Lepidi's strategic assessment of the conflict; it was nearly identical with Drust's.

"War…you think this is a war?"

"Yes, it is a war. I realize that you Romans don't consider the northern tribes worthy enough adversaries to call their conflict with us a war, but perhaps when we beat you back to the south, you will reconsider."

He pulled on the rope again and Lollia's neck stretched. He was using her pain to express his annoyance. She stared at Metella, accusing him of annoying her tormentor. Just before she passed out, he relaxed his grip.

"I will fuck her tonight, Roman, after I whip her of course. She is beautiful, but unskilled in the art of bringing pleasure to a man. I hope to train her in this before she dies. She has a lovely pink asshole—very tight—that I am now working to train. Isn't that right, *Madigan*.

"I have renamed her *Madigan*—dog, because that's what she is to me now, my pet."

Xara raised her eyes but remained silent. Metella could feel her tension—the Romans in Rumabo had apparently kept her chained with their dogs while she matured.

"Did you know that Romans kept your slave with their dogs, that they tortured and killed her parents, destroyed her tribe, and condemned her to the cross when she fought them too well at Wolf's Glen?"

Metella didn't answer. Of course, he knew; he was one of the Romans who had committed these acts, but this was not the time to debate roman policy.

"No one has ever beaten the Roman legions, Drust," Metella said slowly. "No people, no great army, no hoard has ever stood against Rome's might. Rome now rules everyone in the known world from the Orient to the Great Ocean. Do you think the Picts can win here…against the greatest fighting machine the world has ever known?

"And yes, we are ruthless and at times brutal, but Rome is not only about war. We bring civilization—law, government, art, engineering, science, and other things that a simple soldier like me cannot understand."

He paused, Drust was once again reaching for Lollia's rope.

"Join us in this, great chief. Become an ally. You have the leverage now. Rome doesn't want to send more legions to the north. It's too expensive, but it will send them eventually. It cannot afford to lose a campaign of this magnitude. Imagine an army of hundreds of thousands of legionaries, imagine their cavalry, their war machines, their fortifications everywhere. They will grind the Picts into the dirt and march over them."

Drust pulled on the rope again and Lollia lovely mouth opened in protest, but there was no air for her to make a sound.

"My cock is impatient for the legate's daughter and her sweet Roman ass. Come back tomorrow, soldier, and tell me more about Rome. I want to know my enemy. Tomorrow I will tell you why we reject all of Rome's generous gifts, why we will be victorious against your Roman juggernaut."

Metella stood up without Xara's help. That night, they made gentle love, without stimulating pain. The next day, and for the following ten days, Metella went back to talk more to Drust. He and Xara avoided the subject of escaping together.

Drust continued to torment Lollia and even to release a Roman prisoner to report on her torture, but his heart didn't seem to be in it now that the shock value and the ongoing knowledge that he had established that he was delivering daily agony to a Roman patrician.

On his last night in the village, Metella slipped out of his bed. Xara sensed him leaving and opened her eyes in the darkness, but she didn't say anything. This was his choice. In the moonlight, she watched as he cut Lollia from the drying rack and slipped out of the village with her. The dogs, which the village relied on as a first alarm, were silent. Metella had played with them during the day to win their trust.

Drust tried to look surprised that Metella had escaped and taken the girl, but Xara could see that he was staging his reaction. He had wrung all the advantage he could out of the capture of the two girls; and there was nothing more he could gain by killing Lollia. He had known all along, like her, that Metella would never abandon the legion.

***

The centurion and Lollia had run like frightened rabbits for two days, imagining hoards of Picts on their trail. The fact that they had not encountered any had confused Metella, but he welcomed their absence. The last time he had run from Picts, he had been in hand-to-hand combat for days.

He and Lollia stood in the bog on the outskirts of Vindolanda; they could see the fort's walls in the distance. Metella had shared his clothes with the girl, and she had fashioned them into a brief loincloth and halter.

She had changed. Her capture, watching Arria burn, enduring Drust's torture and his cock had affected her in a way that no one could have predicted. She had acquired perspective and humility. During their time together, Metella had come to admire her.

"There's the fort," Metella said. "You will be back in an hour, safe. Be sure you announce yourself to the guards; it would be too ironic to have gone through all this only to die with a Roman arrow in your heart."

"Come with me, Centurion. My father will reverse your conviction and reinstate you in the

legion. It wasn't your fault that Drust caught me in the forest. I ran away against your orders. You were right to order us to stay put. I will speak for you no matter what my mother says. It will be my word against hers, and other witnesses will come forward if I do."

Metella shook his head.

"I am banished, Lollia. There is no coming back from banishment. Your father would not be able to withstand the criticism even if he agreed to retry the case. Go, go now, I will be alright. I can survive on my own."

She knew this was a lie. The Picts had not followed them with the intensity he expected, but that would not last. At some point, they would find him and kill him as an intruder. If he tried to survive in the forest, only a few miles away, the Atrebates would find him and turn him over to the Picts or the Romans. She wasn't sure where their loyalties lay now that they had helped the Picts, but that would not matter. Metella would be too valuable a prize to ignore.

"You must try, Metella. I will remain here. You go to the fort and bargain with them; tell them that you will rescue me from the Picts but only on the condition that they reverse your conviction and reinstate you…at your old rank. What have we got to lose?"

"I have nothing more to lose, but you can lose your life. The Pict's cannot be far behind us. They might be on you before we finish…negotiating. I don't think you have any more value to them as a captive; they will kill you."

"That is a chance I am willing to take, Centurion. I am not leaving you out here to die."

Metella stared at her. This was not the same brat who had demanded that he strangle Arria.

"Turn around then."

She obeyed. He pulled her arms behind and tied them with tough vines he had found. Placing her face down on the moist earth, he raised her legs behind and tied her ankles to her wrists.

"If the Picts find you, they will think that I brought you here by force. If the Romans find you, they will assume you were my unwilling captive. Neither of them will know that we conspired together if they find you tied like this."

"Good luck, Centurion."

***

Metella approached the wall with his arms up and his hands open.

"Centurion…? You're alive…?"

It was Sergeant Tullas, looking down from the wall's battlements astonished. He had testified for the centurion at his trial.

"I will order the gate opened," he said.

"No, don't open the gate, Tullas. I cannot enter. The legion has banished me, remember? I want to speak to the legate; I have news of his daughter."

Tullas turned and immediately dispatched a runner. In a minute, the legate walked onto the catwalk with the prefect, Lepidi.

"You're alive…!" Lepidi exclaimed, defying the stricture against speaking to a banished legionary.

Metella nodded then turned towards Legate Plecio.

"I know where your daughter is, Legate. It's not far from here. I am willing to try to free her and return her to you if you will agree to hear my appeal."

"There is no appeal to a military conviction," Plecio said without conviction. "Unless…"

"Unless there's new evidence," Lepidi finished for him. "Do you have such evidence, Metella?"

"Yes, I do."

"Then I say let him try!" the prefect roared.

He had been quite vocal in his opposition to the centurion's trial, but with Gegania's testimony…

"What new evidence," the legate asked.

"I cannot say, but you have my word as a centurion that it exists."

"His word has always been good enough, Sir. Let him try," Lepidi said.

Plecio turned towards his prefect, the conflict between his duty and his daughter evident on his face.

"You guarantee this, Prefect…? You will support me in this decision…? You will testify to what you heard here, to my thinking that recovering my daughter will weaken the Pict leader's hold on the people, to the correctness of Metella's first trial and conviction?"

"I will, sir."

He turned back to Metella

"Then go, Centurion. Find her and bring her home to us, and I promise you a special-circumstance re-trial based on new evidence."

Metella nodded and turned away. In seconds, the darkness made him invisible. The next evening, he returned with Lollia.

At his retrial in front of the original panelists, Lollia told a different story than Gegania had, claiming that her mother was too distraught at the time to understand what was happening, and not hearing or seeing things the way they were. Gegania refused to give testify or even to appear at the re-trial. This time, in addition to Sergeant Tullas, a dozen legionaries who had witnessed the forest ambush came forward.

Without the support of the legate, *Tribunus Laticlavius* Concerti did not try to influence the decision of the corporal on the tribunal. In the end, he had no choice but to reverse the original conviction, to expunge it from the centurion's record, and to restore Metella to his old rank of Centurion *Primus Pilus*.

***

Drust was strangely unconcerned about Metella's and Lollia's escape. He organized a search party to track them but spent a day giving detailed instructions to the leader. By the time they left the village, Metella and Lollia were nearly at Vindolanda. When he finally met with Xara, the escape was old news.

"Are you planning to leave us as well, Xara?"

"No. my Lord. My life is here now, and my purpose is to kill Romans."

"…And Metella?"

Xara was quiet for a long time. When she spoke, resolve and regret filled her voice.

"You saw what they did to him, my Lord, after he had served them loyally and well for a quarter century. The centurion is a good man, but he is not like other Romans. For the most part, they are mean and shallow; they have become drunk on greed and see conquest as their right. I hated him once and eventually came to love him, but he has made his choice. He chose the legion over me."

"And you…? Would you have gone with him, abandoned your people, your promises?"

"Yes," she answered honestly, knowing the answer could get her killed.

Drust stared at her for a long time then he spoke to her like a chief.

"I will need a fighter like you at my side. I will also need someone who speaks Latin. There will be much to discuss with these invaders as we push them from our land. I have every intention of winning this war."

Xara fell to her knees and put her face in his feet.

"I never surrendered to the Romans…never and I never will. I promise to serve you, my lord, to my death if necessary while you are fighting Rome. This I swear."

Drust nodded, their bargain made. Xara was once again an enemy of Rome.

THE END OF BOOK 2

Read more of She-Wolf in Book 3 of the series… *The War in the North*